BILLIONAIRE'S ISLA

JUDY ANGELO

The BAD BOY BILLIONAIRES Series
Volume 3

ISBN 9798749514506

BAD BOY BILLIONAIRES
Volume 1 - Tamed by the Billionaire
Volume 2 - Maid in the USA
Volume 3 - Billionaire's Island Bride
Volume 4 - Dangerous Deception
Volume 5 - To Tame a Tycoon
Volume 6 - Sweet Seduction
Volume 7 - Daddy by December
Volume 8 - To Catch a Man (in 30 Days or Less)
Volume 9 – Bedding her Billionaire Boss
Volume 10 - Her Indecent Proposal
Volume 11 - So Much Trouble When She Walked In
Volume 12 – Married by Midnight

THE BILLIONAIRE BROTHERS KENT
Book 1 - The Billionaire Next Door
Book 2 - Babies for the Billionaire
Book 3 - Billionaire's Blackmail Bride
Book 4 - Bossing the Billionaire

THE CASTILLOS
Book 1 - Beauty and the Beastly Billionaire

Book 2 – Training the Tycoon
Book 3 – The Mogul's Maiden Mistress
Book 4 – Eva and the Extreme Executive

HOLIDAY EDITIONS
Rome for the Holidays (Novella)
Rome for Always (Novel)

The NAUGHTY AND NICE Series
Volume 1 - **Naughty by Nature**

COMEDY, CONFLICT & ROMANCE Series
Book 1 - Taming the Fury
Book 2 - Outwitting the Wolf
Book 3 – Romancing Malone

COLLECTIONS

Author contact:

www.judyangelo.com
judyangeloauthor@gmail.com

BAD BOY BILLIONAIRE VERSUS REBEL ISLAND BRIDE - AND THE WINNER IS...

Normally shy and reserved, college student Erin Samuels goes to the island of Santa Marta where she breaks out of her shell and does things that shock even her. And, as if that weren't bad enough, she ends up trapped in a marriage by blackmail!

Dare DeSouza is used to women throwing themselves at him and he lumps Erin Samuels in the same category. Gold-diggers, that's what they all are, but this time he has a plan. He sets out to teach Erin a lesson she'll never forget...and ends up learning the greatest lesson of his life.

An island romance that will keep readers guessing every step of the way...

CHAPTER ONE

"Come on, Erin. Just get it over with."

She shook her head and bit her lip. That was easy for Robyn to say. Robyn was the daring one but she'd never done anything like this in her life.

"Go for it," Maria said in support.

Erin could have happily smacked her. Perspiration settled on her brow but it was not from the Caribbean sun that bore down from a cloudless sky. Erin was nervous as hell.

Inhaling deeply she floated her palms on top of the sparkling water of the swimming pool and stared across its length to the knot of men sitting at the pool bar. They were drinking, talking and laughing, their backs to the pool and the swimmers, their lower bodies submerged in water. The pool bar was a popular location and all the concrete stools were taken with a few of the men resorting to standing in the waist high water and leaning on the counter.

"Just do it and get it over with, Erin." That was Tisha talking.

Erin turned to look back at the group and not for the first time since they'd arrived on the island of Santa Marta she wondered what in heaven's name she was doing here with them.

They were like a rainbow coalition – Robyn with her pale freckled skin and copper red hair, Maria with her waist length black hair and Latin features, Tisha with her shoulder-length braids and mahogany skin. And then there was her, with her creamy skin and chestnut-brown hair.

But they were not a coalition by any means. She was the odd one out. They were all from wealthy families, privileged girls who thought nothing of making trips to the islands for sun, sea and sand. She, on the other hand, had only made it here through the generosity of Robyn's parents and their strong suggestion that Erin take a well-deserved break from on-campus work. She'd spent several months with them while in foster care and they'd been very kind. Now, even though years had passed since she'd left, they still insisted on reaching out to her from time to time with small surprises. This trip was a huge surprise.

Robyn had not been pleased at the sudden addition to her travel party but she finally conceded at her parents' insistence. Erin suspected that she'd given in only because she thought she'd found a readymade gopher for the trip.

Now here she was, caught in a stupid dare, one that her sense of fairness would not let her get out of. The other girls had all performed their assigned tasks which ranged from flirting with strangers to kissing the bartender. And although she'd told them she was not interested she'd been roped into the game. Now it was her turn. She refused to kiss anyone but they'd demanded that she meet them halfway – so she'd agreed to the task: select a man, strike up a conversation, and if he asked her out within two minutes of meeting her she'd win the bet. Stupid? Sure, but she was tired of the harassment and the accusation of being a wet blanket. She'd do it and then tell them to leave her the heck alone.

Tisha swam up to her. "I see a real cutie. Check out the blond-haired guy."

Following the girl's finger she stared at the back of a tall, well-built man with spiky hair. As she watched he turned to the man beside him and, laughing out loud, gave him a slap on the back. The blond-haired man seemed friendly enough and probably would not take offense but still, for some reason she had reservations about approaching him. He might like the attention too much.

Surveying the backs of her potential victims Erin's eyes fell on the strong, lean torso of a dark-haired man. He sat with his back straight although he seemed relaxed in every other way. He was sipping a martini and though he often smiled at the jokes of the other men he seemed more reserved, even aloof. This man, clad in hip-hugging black swim trunks, exuded a power which seemed to draw her to him.

Immediately she knew he would be her target. He looked like a serious kind of guy who would just have a normal conversation with her and then let her go. She didn't care if he asked her out or not. She just wanted her task to be over.

And that would be the end of that.

Sucking in a deep breath, Erin began a slow wade through the waist-high water. She never took her eyes off the back of her now chosen prey.

She was halfway across the pool when she heard giggling behind her. Turning, she gave the girls a scathing look. They held their hands over their mouths, still sniggering, but thankfully they quieted down. The last thing she needed right now was distraction.

Slowly, Erin turned and continued her slow march through the water. All right, she was scared but she'd never backed away from a challenge and she certainly wasn't going to start now. More than that, at all costs she wanted to avoid Robyn's sulking. The girl was a whiner and a bully and tonight Erin did not want to deal with the drama.

She was almost there now. She could see the damp hair curling at the nape of her victim's neck. He was laughing, a deep rumble that emphasized his masculinity. Was this a man she could flirt with? She bit her lip and kept walking. Too late to turn back now.

So focused was she on getting to her target that she forgot the curved metal bar that ran underwater behind the stools. She bumped her foot, lost her balance and began to pitch forward toward the man.

She panicked.

Flinging her arms up Erin grabbed for the nearest support, anything to keep herself from falling. That happened to be the dark stranger's shoulder. She pulled him off his stool, throwing him backwards into the liquid blue of the pool. There was a shout and a huge splash and, to her horror, he disappeared beneath the surface.

"Oh, my God, I'm so sorry." Her hands flew to her mouth and she stared wide-eyed as her victim jumped up, coughing, black hair pasted down on his head, water streaming down his face.

Her eyes rose to his face and she took an involuntary step back, suddenly overwhelmed by the sheer height of him. While sitting he had looked tall but now, face to face, he towered over her five feet four inches.

He was still coughing and by now his friends at the pool bar were laughing heartily at his demise. Even her friends' giggles had turned to peals of laughter.

But Erin did not take her eyes off the man in front of her. His black hair curled wetly around his tanned face and the set of his jaw emphasized his square chin. But it was his gray eyes, so unusual in his dark face, that held her gaze. She could not look away. Like a wild cat he was watching her. Now she was the prey. The look on his face made it clear she was in deep trouble.

He took a step toward her and she backed away.

"You want to play, do you?"

Before she could move another inch he caught her wrist and pulled her up against his hard body. She was pressed so close that she could feel the ripples of his stomach muscles against her chest.

When he dipped his head she jerked back and clamped her lips shut. What in the world? Was he trying to kiss her? Was he crazy?

Suddenly Erin felt herself falling backward and as she hit the water she shrieked. It was cut short when she went under but in seconds she was up, coughing and spluttering, glaring at the now laughing man who stood before her.

"You beast," she yelled. "What are you trying to do? Kill me?"

"Two can play, my dear."

His smug expression, his laughing mouth, the amusement in his eyes so incensed Erin that, before she knew what she was doing, her hand flew up to shove him in the chest.

But he was quick, too quick for her. As it went up he grabbed her wrist. Then, staring deep into her eyes, he turned her hand slowly and bent his head to plant a searing kiss in the middle of her palm.

The touch of his lips sent an electric jolt shooting up her arm and through her body.

She snatched her hand from his. With all the haughtiness she could muster she held her head high, turned and pushed through the water and away from the laughing man.

"I'm leaving," she said to the girls, her voice clipped and cold.

To her surprise and relief they followed her out of the pool without protest, saving her the indignity of listening to the man's mocking laughter.

***

Dare watched the curvy brunette leave the pool, her posse of giggling friends in tow. She'd looked very young but she was obviously in charge. Although the smallest in the group, she held herself like a queen and the three girls tripped after her.

"You're getting old, man." His attorney, Ed, slapped him on the back, still laughing. "Normally you don't let them get away that easily. Are you losing your touch?"

He shook his head, still watching the girl's delectable tush in her hot pink bikini as it disappeared around the corner of the pool hut and out of his view. Only then did he turn to Ed.

"No, still on the ball, but you've got to know how far to go with girls like her."

"Girls like her?" Ed raised his eyebrows. "You know her?"

"Don't need to. I know those kinds of girls and that's all that counts."

"Meaning?"

"Didn't you see that was a set up? That was no accident. That girl and her friends were after something."

"Meaning…you."

"I've had enough of them throwing themselves at me to know when there's just another groupie around."

"Somehow she didn't seem that way to me." It was the first time Roger had spoken. He'd done his share of laughing but had made no comment throughout the whole episode. Now Dare's accountant sounded amused but mildly protective.

"Hold up." Dare gave him a hard look. "Don't tell me you're falling for that game. Don't you see it was all a ruse to get my attention?"

"What makes you think-"

Dare held up his hand, effectively silencing the balding man. "I don't think. I know. I heard them giggling back there long before she attacked. I knew they were up to something. I just didn't expect a near drowning."

"I think you have it wrong, senor."

All three men turned back to the counter to a smiling bartender. He was busy wiping glasses but it was obvious he'd been listening and had formed his own opinion, one he was more than willing to share.

"How's that, Danny?" Dare had to hear this one.

"Been observing those girls for the last couple of days and that tiny one who jumped you is as harmless as a kitten."

Dare stared at Danny's wide smile, incredulous. "That kitten almost drowned me."

"Nah, she just tripped. I think she was trying to flirt with you."

"And is that any better, trying to come on to me? I'm sick of being stalked."

"Aw, senor, I should have your problem."

All the men at the bar laughed at Danny's comment and he laughed too, but he was not done.

"It's those other girls you should worry about. For the last two days they've been in the pool daring one another to do all kinds of crazy things." He slid a fresh martini in front of Dare. "Today is the first time I saw the little one get involved. I guess they must have goaded her into it."

Dare was silent for a moment, thinking. He delayed his response by sipping at the drink. Somehow he was not convinced by Danny's defense. But still, he was intrigued.

He could still feel the petite girl's luscious breasts pressed into his chest even though he'd held her for less than two seconds. She was appealing, no doubt about that, and there was something about her that made him want to see her again. But he'd better let go of that feeling, and fast. He wouldn't fall for that trick – again.

"Danny boy, you have a lot to learn." He laughed good-naturedly at the bartender. "Gold-diggers come in all shapes and sizes."

"Dare, I am shocked. This is not like you," Ed said, imitating the voice of an elderly schoolmarm.

Dare couldn't help laughing out loud. But then he got serious. "I have lots of reasons to be like this and it comes from not so pleasant experiences." One in particular, but he wasn't going to go into that with them.

"Let's forget about them and get back to a more interesting topic. Like basketball."

The men got back to their previous conversation and in no time were engrossed in Roger's account of the most exciting basketball final of all time – the Chicago Bulls against Utah Jazz in 1998 when Michael Jordon scored the winning basket in the last minute of the game, locking Utah out and winning 87-86. He'd been there and never tired of recounting his experience.

Dare joined in the conversation at all the appropriate moments but his mind was far away, wondering if he would see that pixie again. After the way his body had reacted to her it would be best if he never did.

CHAPTER TWO

"I can't believe you did it." Robyn's voice was tinged with disbelief.

Erin bit her lip, wanting to shout that it was a stupid thing to do. Instead she shook her head and walked over to the villa's wide bay window that faced the white sandy beach and the brilliant blue sea. The island was beautiful, a paradise on earth, but here she was in the middle of all this beauty and all she was feeling was miserable.

She'd almost drowned a man and had embarrassed herself in the process all in the name of fitting in. Somehow it didn't seem like it had been worth it. And what a man she'd picked. He was obviously not like the fun-loving guys who had fallen prey to her friends' pranks. This one obviously did not appreciate being jumped. She should have known that from his posture. He was no college kid, that was for sure. More like some big shot businessman. A really hot businessman.

Her mind rushed back to the feel of his muscled torso pressed against her breasts and her breath quickened. Even now, just at the memory of it, a delicious shiver coursed through her body.

But the man was a jerk for dunking her like that. Attraction or no attraction, he was the kind of man to stay far away from. She just prayed that for the rest of her week on the island she would not run into him again.

"Come on, Erin. Get out of that funk. Let's take a dip in the ocean." Maria took her by the shoulders and began steering her toward the French doors. "The day is young. We're bound to find some hunks lounging on the beach."

That did it for Erin. She'd had enough of hunks for one day. "You guys go on ahead. I'll just catch up on some reading."

"On spring break?" Tisha huffed in disgust. "You never know when to quit, do you?"

Erin smiled ruefully, not wanting to dampen their high spirit. "Yeah, that's me. Got to get my daily fix or I'll have withdrawal symptoms. You guys go on and have fun. I'll see you later." And before they could object she turned and headed for her bedroom, closing the door firmly behind her.

That evening Erin woke to the sounds of the girls returning from what must have been an exhilarating day at the beach. They were even louder than usual, giggling and screaming as they burst into the villa. Could she survive another three days of this? She wished Robyn's parents hadn't bought the airline ticket for her. She would have gladly remained behind at the college, locked away in the library, absorbed in a stack of books.

She sighed in relief when they didn't bother to knock on her door but instead showered and dressed to go down to the garden for the buffet style dinner that was usually served there. She wasn't hungry and worse, she didn't want to take the chance of running into that man again.

Erin was deep into the history of medieval European art when the girls returned.

"Give it a break, Erin." Robyn walked over to the sofa and grabbed the tome out of her hands. "You do know how to kill a party. Why do you have to study all the time?"

"I'm not studying. For me that's fun reading." Erin forced a smile, not wanting to dampen their mood. "So how was dinner?"

"Good food, like always." Tisha kicked off her sandals and walked over to turn on the TV. Then she flopped down onto the couch across from Erin. "I ate so much fried fish and tacos I feel like I'm going to pop."

"I've got the perfect way to work off all this food." Robyn's eyes sparkled.

Erin's heart sank. What weird scheme was she cooking up now?

"There's a new DJ coming to the resort nightclub. He's from Japan and word is he's really good. Keeps the dance floor hopping, is what I hear."

"Does he play salsa?" Maria swayed her hips to imaginary music.

"He can play anything. All you have to do is request it."

"So what time do we hit the dance floor?" Tisha looked more than interested. She was always one for a good dance party. She could dance all night and not break a sweat.

"What time can you be ready, Erin?" Robyn gave her a pointed look.

"Me? I didn't say I was going."

"You've been hiding out in your room all afternoon and you've been studying on spring break, only heaven knows why. I'm not leaving you in here to take the color of the walls."

"It's okay, I'm fine…"

"No, it's not fine. My dad didn't fly you down here so you can be a drag and spoil all the fun. We're all supposed to be having fun together."

Erin's smile froze and she stared back at Robyn's determined face. She hadn't just thrown that in her face, had she? But one look at the girl's unapologetic glare said that she had, and she was not taking it back.

So that was it. Because Robyn's father had paid for her trip to Santa Marta Erin was beholden to her and was supposed to follow her every command. She was here to make sure Robyn had fun.

Obviously that was what the redhead thought or else she would not be staring back at her so smugly after making a comment like that.

Okay, now she knew where she stood and she could not wait for the week to pass. In the meanwhile she would play along with Robyn's game, humor her if that was what she wanted, then when they got back to Vancouver she would go back to her life on the college campus, far away from Robyn and her demands.

By the time they were ready to leave at about nine o'clock that night Erin felt a little better. She might as well try to have some fun.

After all, she might never have the opportunity to have an island vacation again. She'd spent a lot of time trying to look good. Her normally curly hair had been brushed straight and swept up in a chignon high on top of her head. The new look made her feel sophisticated, confident. She'd picked a black dress with a flared skirt that fell just above the knees and she was wearing her favorite high heeled sandals, the one with the rhinestones on the straps. She might not be the best dressed in the group but she could stand beside any of them.

As they walked along the cobbled pathway leading from their villa to the main building of the tropical resort Erin breathed in deeply, savoring the fruity smell of the flowers that lined the path. It was a balmy, tropical night. The gentle breeze from the ocean wafted over her skin and the sound of the rolling waves was soothing in her ears. Despite the problems, she'd been enjoying her stay on the island and didn't want to think about leaving all this to go back to cold Vancouver just yet.

They knew they were close to the nightclub when they heard the horns, trumpets and steel pans of the island music.

"Hey, I don't know how to dance to that kind of music," Tisha said with a pout.

Maria laughed. "You? You can dance to anything, girl. I've seen you on the dance floor."

Tisha looked pleased and started to sway her hips to the liquid sounds, her gold dress floating around her athletic legs.

"That's not how you do it," Robyn chimed in, obviously determined to turn the spotlight back on herself. "When you do these island dances you have to be real sexy and twist your hips like this."

She started to gyrate in tight circles and soon had her friends dissolving into helpless laughter. Dancing was definitely not one of Robyn's talents.

By the time they entered the nightclub Erin's mood was much lighter, even carefree. The enthusiasm of the girls was rubbing off on her and she was ready to dance.

At first they all four danced as a group, forming a tight little circle in the crowd of people. When the DJ switched from merengue to the steady rhythms of reggae they kept on dancing, bobbing to the sounds of Bob Marley's "We Jammin'".

Tisha really showed her moves when the DJ began to play dancehall music. The deep, gravelly sound of Sean Paul's lyrics filled the room and she began a slow, sexy movement of the hips that had Erin staring in fascination.

The people dancing closest to their group were watching Tisha too and soon they were cheering her on, clapping to the tune of the music while she danced. When the song ended they all clapped and she curtsied cutely in appreciation.

Erin was not surprised when a handsome, honey-colored man approached her friend and asked her for a dance. Tisha gave him a brilliant smile, obviously flattered by his attention, and sauntered off to the other end of the dance floor.

Maria, who loved attention, began a sexy Latin dance, no matter that the music had no Latin flavor at all. She was not used to Tisha usurping her position as the most visible and most attractive member of the group. She wanted to win her position back.

As she danced, her body-hugging red dress glittered under the strobe lights, emphasizing her voluptuous hips and ample curves. Her long hair swayed, tickling her bottom like a scarf of jet black silk.

Maria now began to get the attention she craved, with the crowd giving her the cheers and claps they'd just showered on Tisha. This only spurred her on to more risque moves and Erin stared in surprise as the Latin beauty suddenly dipped to the floor and came back up, sliding her body up the length of a thin, brown-haired man who'd been watching her in fascination. She began dancing close to the man, rubbing against him, teasing him then pulling back only to press into him again.

He was obviously loving it. He slid a tentative arm around her and then as she pressed into him he became bolder, matching her dips and sways with jerky movements of his own.

Soon the crowd closed around the dancing couple. And then there were two. Erin rocked to the beat of the music and smiled over at Robyn, wondering how soon it would be before she found a partner and disappeared, too.

She did not have to wait long. Apparently getting bored with Erin as her dance partner, Robyn gave her a little wave and pushed through the crowd toward the bar. Robyn could never go too long without a drink.

Now Erin was alone. She pasted a fake smile on her face and continued to bob to the music that had suddenly become tedious.

But she couldn't go running off the dance floor like a frightened doe so she stayed there, alone in a sea of people, rocking to the steady rhythm of the music.

When the DJ switched to slow music it gave her the perfect excuse to finally exit the dance floor. She slid through the mass of dancing couples and headed in the direction of the bar. At least Robyn would be there.

But she was not.

Erin's eyes skimmed the bar, searching for the emerald green dress, but it was nowhere in sight. She sighed. Robyn must have found a guy and gone back to the dance floor. She would just have to entertain herself for a while.

"Hey, baby, you look hot."

Erin turned and came face to face with a bespectacled man, probably in his late forties, with receding brown hair and a wide grin.

"Want to dance?"

"I…no, thank you. I'm taking a break right now." Erin smiled as she spoke the words, not wanting to hurt the man's feelings.

"Aw, come on. I saw you on the dance floor. You're a great dancer. Come show me some of your moves."

The man reached out and put a hand on her shoulder and she felt a shudder go through her. He had some nerve. She jerked away from his touch.

"I really don't feel like dancing right now," she said, her voice firm. "I'm thirsty." As she spoke she was sidling away, trying to get closer to the bar and away from the man.

"Oh, so it's a drink you want. No problem, honey. That's what I'm here for. Then we can have some fun." The man reached out again and this time he grasped her upper arm.

"Let go of me." Wrenching her arm from his grasp, Erin lurched backward and came up hard against a man's solid back.

Now look what the idiot made her do. She gave him a withering glare.

"I'm so sorry," she said, turning around to face the person she had stumbled into, and her words of apology died on her lips. The man from the pool. She was staring up into his cool gray eyes and she could see he was not amused.

"Still at it?" he began, brows drawing together in a frown. "Why don't you-"

"Darling, there you are," she gushed, cutting him off.

His frown deepened but before he could say another word she put her arm around his shoulder in a quick hug.

"I'll have that drink now," she said loudly, with a little giggle as she took his arm and tried to turn him back to face the bar.

He did not budge.

Her heart skipped. He was going to blow her cover.

She stole a glance up at his face and his eyes bored into her. She could not read his expression but she knew he was angry.

She made one last try. "A pina colada would be lovely." Erin gave him her best flirtatious smile and her heart melted with relief as a slow if cynical smile spread across his lips.

In one fluid movement he slid off the bar stool and stood before her and for that moment she was very close to him, so close that she could smell the spicy fragrance of his cologne.

She breathed in then gasped as his big hands spanned her waist.

He lifted her effortlessly and set her down on top of the stool he had just vacated. He spun it around so that she was facing the bar then leaned in beside her.

"A pina colada for the lady."

"Coming right up." The bartender gave him a nod and within seconds was sliding a frothy glass in front of her.

Not knowing what to say next, she dipped her head and took the straw between her lips. She sucked the sweet, foamy liquid into her mouth, glad for the way it soothed her parched throat.

Finally, she looked at him. His face was so close she could see the faint shadow on his chin. The slight stubble gave him a rakish air and, for some reason, her breathing became ragged.

"Th…thank you," she said then licked her lips that suddenly felt so dry. She glanced back into the crowd for the man who had made her flee but he was nowhere in sight.

She glanced back at the man from the pool and he was watching her, so intently that she dropped her eyes back to her glass. Her fingers trembled as she cooled her palms on the cold glass. Bending her head, she took another sip of her drink, glad for the excuse to break eye contact with him while her mind raced to find a way to get out of this mess.

"Let's dance."

Relief flooded through her as she realized she would not have to make conversation with this man who probably thought she'd been stalking him. They could dance for a minute and then she would thank him and disappear into the crowd. Then hopefully she would never have to see him again.

Now why did that thought make her heart slide down to her toes?

She slipped off the stool and took the hand he offered. A quiver went through her and she bit her lip.

His was a large hand, warm and strong, and she could imagine such a hand sliding up her body, cupping her breasts in a bold caress.

Erin, stop it. She gave her head a quick shake and focused on her new dance partner as he led her toward the dance floor.

Once she was safely hidden in the crowd Erin gently pulled on her hand, wanting to break contact as soon as possible. To her dismay, instead of releasing her the man pulled her closer to him and began to sway to the sounds of Boyz II Men's 'I'll Make Love To You'.

Erin wanted to resist. She really did. But his hard body felt so good against hers as he held her close, and the music was so sensual that she felt her reserve melt like the ice in her pina colada. She relaxed as the music pulsated around them. She closed her eyes and let him lead, swaying her hips and matching his every move.

His hand slid to the small of her back and a delicious tingle ran all the way up her spine.

Now was the time to thank him for the dance and make a hasty exit but her tongue felt heavy in her mouth. She closed her eyes. She could not speak.

"What's your name?"

Erin jumped. The man had bent his head and his lips were close to her ear, so close that his warm breath tickled the fine hairs on her skin.

"I'm Erin. And…and you?"

"I'm Dare," he said softly into her ear, and the way he said it made her shiver.

Dare. What an unusual name. But it certainly seemed appropriate for this man holding her close on the dance floor, so bold and unapologetic.

The strains of the song died away and Erin took a deep breath. This was her chance. She cleared her throat.

"Thank you for the dance," she began then gasped as the man, Dare whatever his name was, grasped her hand and started walking off the dance floor, pulling her along with him.

She looked around frantically. Where were the girls? She needed to be rescued. Now. Her eyes skimmed the sea of people but in that mass of bodies there was hardly any chance she would find her suite mates.

Tugging her arm, Erin blurted, "Where are you taking me?"

Dare spared her a backward glance. "This place is getting too crowded for me. Let's get out of here."

Get out of here? To where? He was forgetting that they hadn't arrived at the nightclub together.

"Excuse me," she tugged again, "but I'm not going anywhere with a stranger."

The man ignored her.

By this time they were out a side door and onto a terrace surrounded by an abundant tropical garden. Dare let go of her wrist and leaned his shoulder against a cast iron trellis through which flowered vines twisted and coiled. As he lounged he folded his arms across his chest, watching her.

"So what was that about us being strangers?" He gave a dry chuckle. "After all we've shared – a hug, a dance, a dunk in the pool. I thought we were more than that?"

She bit her lip and looked away. She could understand how it all looked. As far as he was concerned she'd been the one doing the pursuing. She could only guess what he must think of her.

She took a deep breath, thinking fast. Should she tell him the truth about the stupid dare or would he think her a crazy college student who would do anything for kicks? Maybe that wouldn't paint her in such a good light but she could at least tell him about the stalker in the nightclub. He would surely understand her actions then.

She opened her mouth to speak and the man chose that moment to reach out and pull her to him. Caught off guard, she tilted into him. He took the opportunity to turn with her then backed her up against the trellis, pressing her into the flowery metal frame.

Dare raised one arm and rested it on the metal bar above her head, effectively trapping her between himself and the wall. His eyes glinted in the moonlight as he stared down at her.

Erin's heart thumped and she swallowed hard. Goodness. How was she going to get out of this predicament in a dignified manner?

"Kiss me."

"Wh...what?"

"That's what you want, isn't it? Now's your chance."

"I don't know what you're talking about." She glared up at him, shocked by his audacity.

"You threw yourself at me twice in one day. I have to reward all that effort. Now kiss me." Dare's tone was commanding. He put a finger under her chin and tilted her face toward his.

Erin's heart pounded. He was going to kiss her. And she wanted it, dear God she wanted it. But she'd always been "the good girl". Did she dare?

She did. When his lips touched hers she did not stop him. She did not pull away. Erin closed her eyes tight and clung to his muscled arms. His lips were hard, unyielding. His arm snaked around her and he pulled her tight against his body, so close that she could feel the rippling muscles of his torso against her breasts.

She kept her eyes closed, not daring to look into those enigmatic gray eyes, not wanting to read what lay in their depths.

Then all coherent thought flew from her mind as Dare softened his kiss, his lips moving sensually over hers, stealing her breath away. Erin leaned into him, her nipples as hard as pebbles, and then she was kissing him back, answering his passion with a fervor that was alien to her. She moaned under the caress of his lips.

Erin trembled in Dare's arms. Her body was responding to him like she'd done with no man before. And as she stood there wrapped in his arms Erin knew she was in deep trouble.

CHAPTER THREE

Slowly, Dare lifted his head and stared down into the dazed eyes of the girl in his arms. What was she doing to him? He'd meant to dominate her, knock her off balance with his kiss. After all, she'd been pursuing him all day. It was time to take her up on what she was offering, maybe even teach her a lesson in the process.

But, to his chagrin, it was he who was caught off guard. The kiss had left him breathless. Damn, was he getting soft?

He released her and put her away from him. Only then did he speak. "I want to see you again. Let's have dinner tomorrow."

Her eyes widened in apparent shock. "Dinner? But...I don't know you."

Dare almost laughed out loud. What kind of game was she playing? Did she take him for a fool? Why else would she have been coming on to him, twice in one day, if she didn't know who he was? He would have respected her more if she'd just been honest.

"Listen, I know enough about you to know that I want to see you again."

"But…"

"No buts. Do you want to see me again?" He knew he was bullying the girl but that was the whole idea. She'd decided to play with fire so it was no fault of his if she got burned.

"Yes." Her voice was a mere whisper, her eyes huge pools of iridescent hazel. On her face was a look of uncertainty tinged with just a hint of anticipation.

Dare chuckled inwardly. The girl was playing temptress but she had a lot to learn. First lesson - don't make your feelings so obvious. With an expressive face like hers she was going to have a hard task succeeding in her chosen role as seductress.

"It's settled then. We'll have dinner tomorrow at Michelangelo's. They have a private lounge where we can eat and talk undisturbed. Seven o'clock. Meet me there."

She opened her mouth then, those soft lips still swollen from his kiss, but he cut her off before she even had a chance to utter the first word. There was no way he was giving her a chance to back out. He'd had a taste of her lips and, dcccivcr though she may be, he wanted more.

He took her by the elbow and turned her toward the pathway. "Come. Let me walk you back to your villa."

"N...no," she said quickly. "No, thank you. I'm fine. I can get back on my own."

He shrugged. "Until tomorrow then. Seven o'clock." He watched her hurry away, heels clicking on the cobbled stones along the lighted path. He had no concern for her safety. He'd made sure security was at its highest level at his resort, with plain clothes security guards patrolling the grounds twenty four hours a day. In his five years operating the resort he'd never had a visitor fall victim to a crime on his grounds. He was determined to keep that record spotless.

Dare DeSouza was an entrepreneur and had been since as long as he could remember. He'd grown up in Michigan and while in elementary school he'd run a candy business, buying bags of candy for a dollar and selling the sweets to his classmates for a quarter a piece. When his home room teacher found out about it he'd had to abandon his enterprise but by high school he'd graduated to selling soda pop and comic books and was raking in a few hundred dollars a week. By the time he started his engineering degree at MIT he was running an online trading company specializing in collectable items, a business which he sold in his senior year for over a million dollars. With this seed money he started yet another business, another trading company that far surpassed the success of the first, and was soon the head of a multi-million dollar operation.

Then he attended a wedding on the island of Santa Marta and was hooked for life. He loved the richness of the island, the verdant pastures and the vibrant green of the tropical foliage. The brilliant blue of the sea and the sky, the cotton white of the clouds, the rich reds of the flora - everything seemed to practically glow with life. He spent a week there and vowed that he would be back.

Next time he visited the island it was for a site visit and on his third trip he signed the documents for the purchase of Sunsational Resort on the northern coast where the best beaches lay. It was family owned but had been neglected due to lack of funds. The couple's children were less than enthusiastic about the hotel business so they were all too happy when Dare offered them over one hundred million for the place.

And then the rebuilding began - renovating, refurbishing and advertising to let the public know the resort was under new management. Sunsational Resort burst back onto the scene and outshone its rivals, soon placing among the top ten resorts in the Caribbean. He expanded to other islands until he had resorts in four additional Caribbean locations. He'd found a winning enterprise and he was loving it.

But that brought with it a host of challenges, fighting off gold-diggers being one of the annoying things he had to deal with. Just a year ago he'd almost been fooled by an expert who tried to convince him to invest millions in a venture that turned out to be phony. Good thing his accountants and attorneys had done their job and reviewed the proposal before letting him sign on the dotted line. If he'd signed he'd have had to hand over millions to a woman whose greatest asset had been her prowess in bed.

And now soon after he'd gotten rid of that one, here was another. A more innocent-looking package, to be sure, but a deceiver just the same. That was the worst part about being a billionaire. Would he ever be able to find a woman who loved him and not his money? The likelihood of that seemed very slim.

He shoved his fists into his pockets, brows furrowed in thought, and headed back toward his own villa. That other gold-digger,

Chantalle Marsden, had escaped his wrath but he had absolutely no qualms about taking out his revenge on this one.

***

By the time Erin pushed open the door and entered the villa she was shaking and it was not from the light breeze that cooled her shoulders. She was shocked and she was scared. Had she just promised to go out on a date with a man she hardly knew? No, correct that. Didn't know at all. She'd met him all of two times, once in a pool, and the other time by a bar. And he'd ended up kissing her! Her heart flipped in her chest at the horror of it all. She, staid and boring Erin Samuels, had been kissed by a total stranger.

What was worse, she had kissed him back. And she had loved every second of it.

Goodness, what had she become? Was it the romantic atmosphere? Was it the fact that she was miles and miles away from Vancouver, ensconced on an island? She'd heard about girls who'd gone wild on spring break but she wasn't like that. She was Erin

Samuels, bookworm, student librarian, Miss Boring. How had she gone from that to this?

Still deep in thought she walked into the bathroom, unzipped her dress and let it fall to the floor. Her underwear followed. She stepped into the shower and turned the spray on her body, letting the water wash over her. She grimaced as the realization came to her. As much as this was against her norm, she knew there was no way she would miss her date with Dare.

It wasn't until late the next day that Erin mentioned her date to the other girls.

"You, Erin?" Tisha squealed. "I can't believe it. Where'd you find a guy to invite you on a date?"

"Tisha." Maria frowned at the laughing girl. "What? Don't you think men notice Erin? She's a pretty girl."

"Yeah, but she's boring. She never wants to do anything fun." Tisha shrieked and jumped out of reach as Maria tried to pinch her.

Robyn was the only one who wasn't smiling. She seemed deep in thought. Finally she spoke. "What did you say his name was?"

"Dare."

"Check out the name," Tisha said. "Dare. If that's anything to go by, he's my kind of guy."

"But not Erin's," Robyn said with a frown. "So you met him at the bar? And you're going out with him just like that?"

"No…I mean, yes." Erin took a deep breath and began again. "He wasn't the one who came on to me. I bumped into him and anyway I'd met him before. At the pool. Remember the guy I almost drowned?"

The three girls gasped as one. "That's the guy you're going out with?" Tisha's voice was high with excitement.

Erin nodded.

"Wow, that's quite a catch," Maria said, her voice low with obvious respect. "You can see that guy's loaded."

Robyn frowned. "How do you know? All he was wearing were swim trunks and a gold chain. I didn't see anything that spelled money."

"No, but it was the way he carried himself." Maria raised her eyebrows. "Even half-naked the man exuded power. Didn't you notice how the men sitting around him practically bowed in respect? The man's big. I just know it."

"And he asked you out…" Robyn's voice trailed off as she stared at Erin. Her face had that distant look again as if there was something on her mind.

Erin frowned, almost sorry she'd brought up the subject. Her suite-mates were acting like it was impossible for a man to want to go out with her. Well, not so much Maria, but the others. Tisha had practically laughed at the idea and Robyn looked none too pleased. Was she jealous? Erin sighed. Anything was possible where Robyn was concerned. If she wasn't the center of attention she was not happy.

"Well, I just wanted you guys to know where I am tonight," she said with false cheerfulness. "Michelangelo's, seven o'clock. If I'm not home by eleven send in the marines."

Tisha chuckled. "Just keep your cell phone on. We're not going to spoil your fun. Just check in with us if you're running…late." She lifted her eyebrows and gave Erin a naughty grin. "You only live once, right?"

Erin felt the heat rise to her face. Abruptly she got up and walked toward the French doors that opened onto the back patio and the pathway to the beach. "I...need some fresh air. I'm going for a walk."

She could hear the chuckles as she slipped outside. They must think her so pathetic. The ugly duckling, finally asked out on a date when they'd been out every night since they got to the island. While the girls made friends she would return to her room each night and curl up in the sofa with a good book. Not that she'd minded. Now, though, she had her chance to prove to them that she was just as desirable as they were.

The day flew by and before Erin knew it the sun had begun to slide down toward the horizon. Her heart did a bunny hop in her chest. This was it. Her first date while on spring break.

She dressed carefully, picking out a simple yet elegant black dress. She accessorized with a pearl necklace and matching earrings then slipped her feet into high heeled sandals. Now it was time for her hair and face. As she usually did when trying to look sophisticated she took a firm brush to her curls then pinned her hair up into a neat bun. The face was more challenging. She wanted to look good but doing makeup had never been her strong point. She tried some eye shadow and hated it. She had no clue what she was doing and didn't want to ask any of the girls. She'd been humiliated enough for one day. In the end she gave up and settled for foundation, lip gloss and eyeliner. If her date didn't like her that way then that was his problem.

Then it was time to go. She'd been finding all sorts of excuses to dawdle - she couldn't find her purse, she needed another glass of water, she had to redo her lip gloss - until it was ten minutes before the hour. Now she'd have to hurry to make it to Michelangelo's on time. She could see that Dare was not the sort of man who'd take kindly to being kept waiting.

When Erin stepped into the lobby of Michelangelo's she took a deep breath and clutched her purse tightly in her hands. She peered down the dimly lit hallway toward the salon then breathed a sigh of relief. He wasn't here yet. Her racing pulse began to decelerate toward normal.

"Good evening, Erin."

She jumped then whipped round to peer into the darkness of the hallway. And there he stood, tall and imposing in an elegant dinner jacket of dark gray. Those piercing gray eyes glittered in the dim light and she felt as if his gaze stripped her bare.

"Dare," she said, her voice breathless, "I didn't see you over there."

"I know you didn't. Come." He gave her his arm. "A table is reserved for us."

She rested her hand on his arm and as she did so a shiver ran through her. Furtively, she glanced up at him through her lashes. Had he felt it, her body's reaction to his? She hoped he hadn't. That was just what she would need - her body making its response to him unmistakably clear. She breathed a soft sigh of relief when he gave no indication that he'd felt it. He simply kept on walking, her hand tucked into the crook of his arm.

The maitre d' bowed low, showing extreme deference to Dare, then directed them to a private room adjoining the restaurant, an elegantly decorated room aglow with the soft light of a dozen candles shining through stained glass shades that lined the walls. In the middle of the table was what looked like a bouquet of flowers but turned out to be flower shaped candles from which an almost heavenly fragrance wafted.

Dare released her arm and pulled out her chair then he went to sit across from her, his eyes never once leaving her face. It was if he was seeing her for the first time, so intense was his stare. Or was there something more? There was a gleam in his eyes, one that she could not decipher. The only word that came to mind was 'wicked'. She could feel her breathing grow shallow. Goodness, had she made a mistake in coming?

But then inexplicably his demeanor changed. Gone were the frown that had darkened his face, gone was the intense stare that was almost a glare, and in their place was a half-smile that, while not totally reassuring, made her breathing just a little bit easier.

Dare took charge, placing the order for both of them. He seemed familiar with everything on the menu so there was no need to question his recommendation.

In fact, just then Erin was feeling so out of her depth she doubted she would have been able to order anyway. She wasn't even sure she'd be able to eat when the meal arrived. Dropping her hands to her lap she twisted her napkin with shaking fingers and pasted a bright smile on her face.

"Are you all right?" Dare's frown was back. He was watching her intently, his gray eyes glittering like shards of glass in the candlelight.

"I'm…fine, thank you." The words came out stilted and strained. She swallowed and tried again, hiding desperately behind her fake smile. "This is a really nice place. It seems to be the nicest restaurant at the resort."

"I like it." His voice was brusque and cool. It was almost as if he had no interest in conversation.

Confused, Erin bit her lip. Why had he asked her to dinner? He was acting like she was an annoyance.

She dropped the napkin onto her lap, lifted her head and looked him squarely in the eyes. Enough was enough. "You didn't really want to invite me out, did you?"

"Excuse me?" He straightened, obviously caught off guard by her direct question.

"This…date, if you can call it that. Clearly, you don't want to be here so why did you invite me out?" Erin gave him her coldest stare.

"I'm…sorry," he said, his voice low. He had the decency to look contrite. "I've had a rough day and was a bit…distracted." He leaned forward and for the first time that evening he gave her a smile that could be described as warm. "That's no excuse for my behavior and I'm sorry. Forgive me?" He gave her a puppy dog look that melted her heart.

How could she say no? She smiled back at him. "Of course," she said with a slight nod of her head and when he reached out and took her hand she did not pull it away.

After that the rest of the date went smoothly and soon Erin began to relax in Dare's company. He was charming and witty, and she found herself laughing at his insightful and satirical observations on life. She was seeing another side to this man she'd branded as too domineering and too bold. He actually had a sense of humor.

She'd just finished her second glass of wine when the server approached the table, bottle at ready. This time she quickly covered her glass with her hand.

"I'm fine, thank you," she told him with a smile.

"Are you sure?" Dare asked and a mischievous smile played on his lips. "You're on vacation, remember? No time like the present to let your hair down."

She thought about it. He was right. It was not like she had to drive a car afterwards so no fear of DUI. And she didn't have to get up next day to head out to work or classes. What harm could one more glass of wine do? Besides, she liked wine.

She began to slide her fingers away, her lips slightly pursed in anticipation of the tangy liquid, but then her better self, good old cautious Erin, came to the rescue. "No," she said, shaking her head. "I rarely drink so two glasses of wine is enough, I think. I'll have to walk back to the villa, remember?" She was looking at Dare and gave a little laugh as he gave her an exaggerated look of disappointment. Then when he gave her a pout and wiped away a fake tear she laughed out loud. Dare DeSouza was actually a funny guy.

Seeming satisfied that he'd made her laugh, Dare turned to the server. "Just one glass, please. We'll share it."

At his words Erin's eyes widened and she felt the warmth of a blush rise to her face. We'll share it? Whoa, hold on. Wasn't that much too intimate for two people who hardly knew each other? She continued to stare at Dare, trying to look composed, but she could feel her smile faltering.

Within an instant a fresh glass of white wine was placed on the table between them and the server slipped discreetly away. Erin tore her eyes from Dare's face and looked instead at the sparkling liquid.

He chuckled and reached out a hand to slide the glass closer to her. "You first," he said and the way he said it was both commanding and seductive at the same time.

For a moment Erin hesitated. Then the tension in her dissipated. She relaxed and reached for the glass. She wasn't going to have all of it, after all. She picked it up by its delicate stem and lifted it to her mouth, her eyes never leaving Dare's sharp gray ones. She took a small sip then another and another until Dare stopped her with a laugh.

"Hey, leave some for me. We're supposed to be sharing, remember?"

She laughed too, and lowered the glass to the table then slid it across to him. She was staring at him, she knew, but she couldn't help it. His smile so transformed his face that she could hardly believe he was the same man, the cold, hard brute she'd met the day before. He now looked something very close to a naughty boy planning some devious trick.

This time it was Dare's turn to put the glass to his lips. He gave it a slight turn with his fingers, seeming to deliberately position it so that his mouth would fall precisely where hers had been just moments before. Then, before Erin could guess what he was about to do, his tongue darted out to taste the memory of her lips.

Erin's breath caught in her throat. A simple gesture was all it had been but never had she seen anything more erotic. He'd sent her a clear and unmistakable message without saying a single word. Dare DeSouza wanted her in no uncertain terms.

Her pulse racing Erin watched, mesmerized, as Dare took a sip and another, then his tongue slipped out again this time to catch a stray drop of wine from his lips. But he did it so slowly, so sensually, she knew it was all for her.

He was obviously intent on seducing her and it was working. She drew in a deep breath, trying her best to calm her racing heart, but it was difficult to stay serene when the sexiest man on the island was coming on to her. Goodness, nothing she'd experienced in the past had prepared her for this.

Another sip and Dare had finished the glass of wine. Now he turned all his attention on her. He leaned forward and took her hands in his big strong ones.

When he looked down at them she closed her eyes, willing her hands not to tremble. *Come on, Erin, you're a big girl. You can handle this.* The best way to handle it was to distract him in some way.

"Umm, why don't we go for a walk? It's a nice balmy night." She glanced at him, hopeful that he would take the bait. She needed to get away, out of this intimate space where they were all alone and he could seduce her wickedly without prying eyes. Out in the open he would have to behave. She hoped.

He did not object. "We might as well walk off some of this food. Come." He quickly signed the bill and rose, and as he'd done before he gave her his arm.

Erin stifled a smile. The consummate gentleman when he wished to be. But she was not fooled. Underneath that polished exterior was a man who could be as hard as iron. She'd seen it in his unforgiving response to her blunder in the pool. She'd felt it in his punishing grip when he'd thought she was about to flee. And she could sense it now, as he stood tall and imposing, looking down at her with those steel-gray eyes. She took his arm, thankful to be leaving the romantic atmosphere behind. She needed all her wits about her when dealing with this man and the combination of the fragrant candlelit room and two and a half glasses of wine were not helping.

She sighed with relief as they left the restaurant behind and set off along the cobbled pathway. For a while they walked in silence under the moonlight, breathing in the perfume of the frangipanis that lined the pathway and listening to the sounds of music and laughter in the distance. It was a romantic night, with stars winking in the deep velvet of the sky, and Erin could almost imagine they were lovers enjoying the night and each other's company. If only it were true.

They'd been walking almost aimlessly for some time before Erin realized they'd left the cobblestones and were now on sandy soil. Her stiletto heels had begun to sink into the soft earth and she suddenly found herself toppling over.

With a laugh Dare caught her to him and then without warning his mouth descended and he was kissing her with a passion that left her clinging to him, breathless. Before she could recover Dare bent and swept her legs from under her, lifting her up into his arms.

Erin squealed in shock and then in delight as he swung her round then strode purposefully along the dirt path. When she looked over his shoulder she realized he'd taken her down to the beach where the waves were rolling in to break against the shore.

"Dare," she whispered, almost afraid she would disturb the steady rhythm of the ocean, "what are you doing? We can't be down here."

He chuckled, a low throaty rumble that echoed in her ear as her cheek pressed against his chest. "We can, my precious, and we are. It's the perfect night to be on the beach."

They got to a long, low palm that stretched toward the ocean and in its shadow Dare laid her on a soft bed of grass.

And there he began his sweet, sensual assault.

He started with a kiss that made her tingle all the way down to her toes. Then his lips were sliding down her neck to the valley between her breasts.

"Dare," she gasped and she could say nothing more, her nipples so eager for his lips that they ached. What was this man doing to her? He was being deliberate and slow, teasing her to a degree of desire she had never felt before.

As his breath warmed her flesh Erin moaned and shifted on her bed of grass, wanting to give him more access to her body.

Dare needed no further invitation. To Erin's relief and delight he slipped his arm behind her arched back and as her breasts thrust upward he slid her top away and captured a turgid nipple between his teeth.

Shockwaves of ecstasy rippled through her and an involuntary moan escaped her lips. She reached up with trembling hands and slid her fingers into the dark thickness of his hair then she was clinging to him, pulling his head down, and begging him for release from his slow, sweet, torture of her breast.

Dare took pity on her when he released her tingling nipple and replaced his teeth with his lips, suckling and soothing until she writhed with want.

Under his expert hands Erin felt like her very bones had melted. She was without the power to resist his hands, his lips, and his tongue. There on the warm sand under a sky filled with perfect stars she was lost to him.

"Come. Let's head back to the villas."

His words jerked her out of her heavenly trance. What? Was he stopping? Now? Her eyes fluttered open. She stared up at him, confused, but with his face hidden in the shadows she could find no answers there.

Then he was reaching out his hands to her and helping her to her feet, and as she was rising to stand beside him her heart was sinking down to the sand.

She kept her head down, unable to meet his eyes. For some reason she could not understand he'd changed his mind. He didn't want her anymore. He would walk her back to her villa and that would be that.

Maybe it would all be for the best. She'd been out of her depth, anyway. Then why did she feel so devastated?

Even though Dare continued to hold her hand for the entire walk back to the villas Erin kept her face averted, determined not to let him see her disappointment. She was so caught up in her own feelings that she was surprised when they came to a halt. Were they at her villa already? She looked up then lifted her brows in surprise. This wasn't her villa at all. This one was huge, the largest she'd seen at the resort, and it was magnificent with tiles of black marble gleaming in the light cast by the lamps at the entrance.

Erin hung back, hesitant. "Where…are we?" she whispered, looking around.

"Come," Dare, said with a reassuring smile. "We'll be more comfortable here."

He slid his card into the slot and pushed the door open. Then right there in the open doorway he pulled her into his arms and kissed her with an ardor that left her panting.

His kiss wiped all thoughts, all concerns from her mind. All she wanted was to lose herself in the powerful arms of this man whose charm had swept her off her feet. Then, just like he'd done before, he lifted her off her feet, slammed the door shut with his foot and headed across the foyer and down the hallway.

Erin's heart pounded in her chest. She was no idiot. She knew what Dare wanted and God help her, she wanted it, too. She bit her lip and pressed her face to the soft fabric of his shirt. She could feel the blood rush to her face, she could almost taste the fear, but she would not stop him. Tonight she might be making the biggest mistake of her life but she wanted this too badly to care.

Still holding her close, Dare reached down and opened the door to a massive bedroom lit by a lone lamp standing in the far corner. He strode across the room and laid her on the bed then before she even had a chance to move he'd caught hold of the hem of her dress and was sliding it over her hips and up till she had to shift so he could pull it over her head. Left in only black lace bra, matching panties and stilettos Erin could only shiver under his heated gaze.

To her shock and her body's delight Dare leaned over to plant a kiss on the softness of her belly then he was sliding his lips down, down until she gasped in anticipation.

He lifted his lips then, and there was a smile on his face and a twinkle in his eyes. "Not yet, my sweet," he whispered. "Patience."

He straightened and, with deft fingers, he unbuttoned his shirt, never once taking his eyes off her. His bare chest, so broad and muscled, gleamed golden in the light of the lamp. Next to go was his belt then his shoes, socks, and trousers until the only thing hiding his nakedness from her was thigh-length briefs that did little to conceal his straining bulge.

A wave of embarrassment washed over Erin and she was just about to turn her face away when he hooked his thumbs into the waistband and pushed the garment off his hips and down his legs. Too late. No time to avert her eyes. She could not have looked away if her life depended on it, so mesmerized was she by the sight of his nakedness, his manhood so rigid with want.

He came to her then, sliding onto the bed with her, covering her lips with a kiss that stole her breath from her. And while he kissed her senseless his hands slid down to unhook her bra and free her tingling breasts to the caress of his hands. He released her lips just long enough to divest her of panties and high heels and then he was sliding the solid length of his body up her nakedness and back to her waiting lips.

   ***

After he'd had his fill Dare broke the kiss and slid off the bed to grab his trousers. He pulled a condom from his wallet and ripped the packet open with his teeth. As he sheathed himself he stared down at the girl lying on his sofa, her eyes tightly closed, her teeth biting down on her lower lip. What the hell kind of game was she playing?

She'd rolled with him every step of the way, flirting with him in the restaurant, coming back to his villa, kissing him with an eagerness that was ample evidence of her desire. And she'd said she wanted this.

Now she was acting like some sort of vestal virgin who'd never done this before. Maybe it was an act. Did she think ravishing inexperienced maidens was his fetish? He almost laughed out loud. He knew girls like her. Tease - that was what they called them. Well, she'd better get ready for the teasing of her life.

Dare returned to the bed where he slid his hand along her thigh then up to her mound where he began to stroke and tease. He was getting her ready for him.

She moaned and her legs began to part for him but still she kept her eyes closed.

It was only when he moved up and over her that her eyes flew open and as he stared into those brown eyes so cloudy with passion he positioned his hips over hers and sank deep inside her.

Erin stiffened and there was a momentary flash of something akin to panic but then she closed her eyes again, shutting him out, hiding from him the depth of her soul.

Unfazed, Dare dipped his head and brushed her ear with his lips. He smiled when she moaned in response. He had supreme confidence in his ability to stoke the embers of passion in this woman. She would not be passive in his arms.

For a whisper of a moment he lay still, giving her time to adjust to his entry, and then he was moving, thrusting slowly at first then more forcefully as she writhed in his arms. When she gasped and clung to him the fire inside him flared up and trapped his breath in his lungs, making him gasp for air.

Soon it was his body that was in control and he was thrusting toward his peak, driving into her until all his lust, passion and desire exploded inside her, leaving him panting and drained.

He looked at her then and what he saw made his breath catch in his throat. She was staring up at him, her eyes misty with tears, and she was smiling. Had it been as good for her as it had been for him? It had been sweet, too sweet in fact. He'd peaked a lot quicker than normal. There was something about this girl that drove him to distraction, made him lose his cool. But not to worry. The night was still young and he planned to drink his fill of her, get her out of his system then purge her for good. By the end of the night Miss Erin Samuels would know not to mess with the big boys.

***

The sun was just peeping out on the world and the birds were beginning the morning's serenade when Erin woke to feel warm hands on her breasts. Eyes still closed, she sighed and turned to give Dare greater access to her and when he replaced his hands with his lips she moaned beneath his caress.

They made sweet love that morning and although her body ached from the vigor of Dare's attention, it was a pleasing ache that came with a feeling of total satisfaction. She'd never experienced anything like this in her life.

When he turned his head on the pillow and looked over at her she felt the blush rise in her face. She'd actually spent the entire night in this man's bed. Who would have thought that she'd have had the courage? She, who had avoided men like the plague? She felt a giggle rise in her throat as her thoughts went to her roommates. They would rib her mercilessly when she got back. Her first 'sleep over' with a man. She could hardly believe it herself. She would just have to put this down to 'island fever'.

But it was more than 'island fever'. Since the day they met there was something about Dare that had drawn her to him. Maybe that was why she'd picked him out of all the men at the bar. It was almost as if she'd had no choice in the matter. And then they'd had this night together. This wonderful, wonderful night. At first she'd been scared but then she'd relaxed in his care, feeling that for the first time in her life she'd found a man she could trust.

She was still curled up beside him in the bed, lost in her thoughts, when Dare's voice pulled her out of her reverie.

"Well, you've served your purpose. Time to go."

At Dare's words Erin's eyes snapped back into focus and she stared up at him. "Excuse me?"

"Time to go," he said again. He leaned back on his pillow and locked his arms behind his head in a gesture of relaxation. "You wanted a taste of a billionaire and I wanted a taste of you. We both got what we wanted so now it's time for you to get out."

Dear God, what was he saying? Eyes wide, Erin clutched the sheet to her breasts and sat up. "Are…are you throwing me out?"

She held her breath, praying he would burst out laughing and tell her he'd been pulling her leg. But no, to her horror he was nodding, a smug expression on his face.

"Yep," he said and this time he did laugh but it was a bitter laugh that sounded mean and ugly to her ears.

"I know girls like you," he said, his voice harsh and brittle as brass, "gold-diggers on the lookout for the richest man they can find. You get him to sleep with you, get him to fall for you and then you take him for all he's got." He chuckled. "I'm on to your game, babe. This is one rich dude you're not going to take for a ride."

The blood turned to ice in Erin's veins. If he'd hauled off and slapped her across the face she could not have been more shocked. Or hurt. Or devastated.

She now realized the truth. Dare, this man she thought she had come to know, had never been attracted to her. He'd never felt anything for her. All he had wanted was to get her into his bed, use her, and then toss her away like disposable dinnerware.

Heat rushed to her face then drained away leaving her cold and shivering and dazed. Then as the chill of his words encircled her heart, turning it into a solid block of ice, she dropped the covers, no longer caring, and stumbled out of the bed. Almost blindly, she fumbled around on the floor reaching for her bra under the chair, her panties under the bed and her dress, now a crumpled mass of black silk on the floor. It looked like exactly how she felt – trampled, damaged and discarded.

With a sob she kneeled on the floor and put on her panties and bra then pulled the dress over her head. Her purse and her shoes were nowhere to be seen.

Slowly she got up and walked on unsteady feet across the room. She wanted to cry. She wanted to throw herself on the floor and bawl. But she would not. She would never give this man the satisfaction of knowing how much he had hurt her. Even though she was dying inside she lifted her chin and without a backward glance she walked out of the room.

She found her shoes and purse in the living room. She retrieved them and then she walked out of Dare's villa and out of his life.

***

A heel. That was what Dare felt like as he lay on the bed staring up at the ceiling. It had been over twenty minutes since Erin left his villa and still he had not moved. The look on the girl's face, the sight of her dejection had floored him.

Had he made a mistake? Had he been wrong in how he'd judged her? It couldn't be. She'd come on to him at the pool and just like he'd expected she'd found a way to conveniently bump into him again, this time at the bar. She'd even jumped at his invitation to dinner. And even more telling, she'd had no objection when he had taken her to his place. She'd given him every indication that she was after something and he'd been right to cut her loose.

Then why did he feel so low? Was it because of the panic he'd seen in her eyes? Was it the way she'd clung to him each time they made love? Was it the hurt he'd seen in her eyes?

Dare shook his head. No, she couldn't be feeling hurt at his rejection. Anger, maybe. Disappointment. But not hurt. She'd gone into this with her eyes wide open, knowing the risk of trying to seduce a man. She must have been prepared for either outcome.

This was what his brain was telling him. He just wished that other side of him, that weaker part that dealt with his emotions, would just shut up and accept. He'd been right in doing what he did.

The girl needed to pay.

So why did he feel like such a jerk?

CHAPTER FOUR

It was just after six in the morning when Erin sneaked into the villa, quiet as a cat, and hid herself in her bedroom. Thank God the girls were still fast asleep.

She went into the bathroom and locked the door and there, in the privacy of that space, she slid down to the rug on the floor, hid her face in her hands, and wept.

She had never been so humiliated in her life. To think that she had trusted this man, had felt an emotional connection with him, and then he'd turned out to be the same as the jerks she'd known all her life. She would never trust a man again. Life was infinitely better when she was alone.

With a sniff, Erin got up from the floor. She stepped out of her shoes then stripped off her dress and underwear, removing from her body all memories of the night before. From here on Dare would be a distant memory, just someone stored away in her collection of experiences. That was all. She stepped into the tub, turned on the shower and submerged herself in the cleansing flow.

Erin was relieved when the girls got up later that morning and seemed to have forgotten about her date. They must have come in late last night, half drunk as usual. They seem to have totally forgotten that she'd even gone out. Only Robyn seemed to be regarding her with some interest. Finally, as Erin was packing the plates back onto the room service trolley, she spoke.

"So," she said, dragging out the word as she eyed Erin from across the room, "how did it go with lover boy last night?"

"L…lover boy?" Erin's heart sank as she realized she hadn't escaped. Robyn wanted answers and what Robyn wanted Robyn got.

"Yeah, your date. What? Did it bomb?" The girl looked almost eager to hear bad news.

"Yes. Yes, it did." Erin seized on the direction the conversation had taken. All Robyn wanted to know was that she'd had a terrible time and then she'd leave her alone.

"Aww, that's too bad." Tisha went over and put her arm around Erin's shoulder. "Don't let it get you down, though. We can still have some fun tonight."

Tonight. For her there would be no fun. It would be their last night on the island before heading back to Vancouver and she planned to spend it hidden away in her room.

If she'd spent her time as she normally did, alone and lost in an art history text, she would not have fallen into the trap set by the devil himself. She'd learned her lesson. Home was the safest place to be.

She said none of this out loud, though. She kept her thoughts to herself and pasted a brave smile on her face. "Sure," she said brightly. "There's always tonight."

After breakfast Maria, Tisha and Robyn went down to the beach to take advantage of their last opportunity to tan under the hot Caribbean sun and dip in the ocean. It was also their last chance to preen in front of the many available college guys who had come to the island looking for fun. When they'd hounded Erin to come along she had flatly refused. She would not risk running into Dare again.

As long as she stayed in the villa she would be safe. Thank goodness she'd never told him her last name. He would have no way of finding her. Not that she thought he'd be looking. She had absolutely no desire for him to even consider looking for her. That was what she told herself but the puddle of pain at the pit of her stomach was testament to the lie she'd been feeding herself. She was hurting and there was no denying that.

After a night of packing and contemplation Erin left the Island of Santa Marta early the next morning relieved that she would never lay eyes on this confounded place again.

***

From her seat in the crowd of black-gowned students Erin looked over at the sea of faces - friends, family and well-wishers who had come from far and near to celebrate the special occasion. Within less than an hour the ceremony would be over and each graduate would leave, ready to move on to the next stage in life.

Erin was smiling as she watched the happy faces but even as she celebrated with her batch mates she couldn't help feeling a twinge of sadness. How she wished she had someone, anyone, to celebrate with her.

There'd been a day when she'd had a mother and a father who loved her dearly. They would have been here today to share in this rite of passage but it had been nine years since they'd been torn from her life, the victims of a motor vehicle accident caused by a drunk driver.

With her only living relative being an aunt who lived and worked in South America as a missionary Erin had ended up in foster care, moving from family to family from the age of twelve until she was eighteen.

She'd won her freedom then. By working hard throughout high school she'd won a tuition scholarship to a college of her choice and now, four years later and with thousands of hours of part-time work under her belt, she'd made it. Now to face the real world. She was eager to step over that threshold and start making some real money.

Armed with her degree in liberal arts Erin sent out resume after resume to museums, government agencies, schools and non-profit organizations, hopeful that she would land a job within a few weeks. She had enough money to last her about a month and a half. So this was what it felt like to be just one paycheck away from the homeless shelter. She had to find a job and fast.

But things did not go as Erin planned. Three weeks into her job search she still had not been called for a single interview. It was all due to the recession, the career office told her, coupled with the fact that the market had just been flooded with thousands of new graduates competing for the few limited job openings. Erin acknowledged that might all be true but that knowledge didn't help her situation, now only about three weeks away from starvation. And how was she going to pay next month's rent?

And if that weren't bad enough she'd suddenly been attacked by a stomach virus. Two days in a row she'd woken up to a bout of nausea and had had to rush to the bathroom where she'd emptied the contents of her stomach. When the third day turned out to be more of the same Erin knew she had to make the sacrifice and dip into her meager savings to get the money to visit a doctor. Her college health insurance coverage had expired so all medical costs were now her responsibility.

At the medical clinic she grudgingly handed over the eighty-dollar fee then went to sit in the waiting lounge. She picked up the latest copy of Cosmopolitan then put it down again, unable to concentrate. There was just too much on her mind. There were so many things she needed to do. She needed to start pounding the pavement, she had to find a job. Dear God, how was she going to survive?

She glanced at her watch for the fifth time. Why hadn't the doctor called her yet? She couldn't afford to waste all this time just sitting around. She had to get back to her job hunting. Unable to sit still any longer she got up and went over to stare at the goldfish swimming serenely in their colorfully decorated house of glass. She envied them.

"Ms. Samuels?"

At the sound of her name Erin turned to see the medical assistant standing in the doorway, smiling at her. She gave a sigh of relief. Finally.

Dr. Saunders greeted Erin warmly and listened attentively as she described her ailment. After a quick check of her blood pressure, heart and lungs he gave a nod. "Everything seems to be in order. Will you have a seat, please?"

She slid off the examination table and went back to sit in the chair across from the doctor's desk.

"Ms. Samuels," he said with a gentle smile, "is there any possibility that you are pregnant?"

"Preg…pregnant?" The words came out in a shocked whisper.

"Yes, pregnant," the doctor said patiently. "Are you sexually active?"

"N…no. I mean, yes. I…" she could not go on. Pregnant? The thought hadn't even crossed her mind.

"So which is it?" the doctor chuckled but there was no sign of judgment on his face. "I need you to do a pregnancy test today. If it's negative we'll run some other tests but let's start there."

In a daze Erin took the lab requisition from the doctor then with a nod of thanks she turned toward the door. Could she really be pregnant?

As she sat in the waiting room she relived the night she'd spent in Dare's arms. Three times they'd made love and all three times he'd used a condom. They'd been careful. Pregnancy could not be the cause of her problems. She began to breathe a little easier at the thought. Then she thought back to the last few months since she'd left the island. She hadn't had a period since her return but that was normal for her. She was one of the lucky souls who only had a period three or four times a year. Her gynecologist had told her it would in no way affect her ability to have children so she hadn't been concerned. Until now.

The gravity of the situation was like a slap to the face. If she were really pregnant how in heaven's name was she going to manage? She could barely feed herself let alone a baby. And where would they live?

She covered her face with her hands, trying to control her emotions. It would not do to burst into tears right there in the middle of the waiting room. But, dear God, what was she going to do?

It took only thirty minutes for Erin to receive the verdict. She was indeed pregnant. And she was expected to give birth in twenty-four weeks. With that news her world crumbled around her.

Erin spent the rest of the afternoon feeling sorry for herself. Then, as she always did when facing a crisis, she began to plan her course of action.

First, she had to find a way to start earning money immediately. Looking for jobs in her field of study was not working and it didn't make sense to continue down that path. She would set her sights lower, take anything she could get, just as long as it was available now and provided a steady income. Next, she would move to a smaller place, probably somewhere farther away from the college since apartments in that area tended to be more expensive due to the high demand. She would probably even have to seek a roommate. She wasn't thrilled at the idea but under the circumstances she had no choice.

Then she would start checking out the thrift stores. As much as she hated the idea of dressing her baby in recycled clothing it was better than no clothes at all. She sighed and sat down to write her list. A crib, bedding, clothes and a stroller. At minimum she would have to have those. Oh, and a baby car seat. She'd need that the day she took him…or her…from the hospital. Even if she told them she'd be taking a taxi home the hospital staff would never let her leave without a car seat for the baby.

Her plan in place, Erin began to pound the pavement. Literally. Next day she was up with the sun. She'd dressed carefully, applied a little make-up, and with her resume adjusted to suit the marketplace she took the bus to the heart of the city and began to walk. She'd printed one hundred copies of her resume and before the week was out she planned to have dropped off every one of them.

By the end of the first day Erin had submitted applications at twenty-one establishments including Subway, Mc Donald's, Whole Foods and Tim Horton's, the most popular coffee shop chain in the country. She knew that if she was lucky enough to get a call from one of them the pay would be small, probably little more than minimum wage, but at least most of the restaurants offered employees free meals. Food was one thing she wouldn't have to worry about.

Next day Erin was out again by seven in the morning. She didn't get back home until the sun had already set. Still, she was satisfied she'd beat the previous day's record, submitting twenty-five applications that day. By the end of the third day she'd reached sixty-six in total. Completely exhausted, she only had the energy to shower and climb into bed with a prayer that her hard work would soon bear fruit.

The fourth day dawned and despite the feeling of nausea that attacked her Erin pulled on her walking shoes and headed out to begin her daily trek. She didn't feel as energetic and her spirit had begun to flag. Still, she pressed on, knocking on every door where she felt there was any possibility of her finding work.

She was speaking with a receptionist at a small family restaurant when her phone rang.

"Excuse me." She gave the woman an apologetic smile and turned away to take the call. "Ms. Samuels?" It was a male voice, deep and gravelly and very formal.

"Yes, this is Erin Samuels." Her heart leaped in anticipation. Was this the good news she'd been praying for before?

"This is Mike Mason from Benny's Restaurant. You dropped off an application on Monday." There was the sound of papers shuffling in the background. Then he continued. "I was wondering if you could come in to meet with me tomorrow?"

"Yes, of course," she said, breathless. "What time would you like me to come in?"

They made the arrangements then Erin slid the phone shut. Her first interview. At the thought her face broke into a wide smile. She couldn't help it. Thank you, God.

Then, remembering where she was, she quickly composed herself and walked back to the reception desk where she proceeded to enquire about job openings. She had to keep searching. Who knew what tomorrow would bring? She was keeping her fingers crossed that she'd nail it. But until then she would keep on looking.

Next day Erin arrived ten minutes early for her first interview. She'd worn her navy blue power suit and her curly hair was pulled back into a neat bun. She announced herself to the greeter who invited her to a small office where she could wait for Mr. Mason.

Perched on the edge of her chair with her purse clutched tightly on her lap Erin surveyed the room. It was a small, neat office with very little furniture except for a huge antique desk that dominated the room. The restaurant, too, had been neat and clean. She'd observed that as she was following the girl to the office. She liked that. The place had a homely atmosphere that made her feel almost comfortable, as if she worked there already and had been doing so for years.

"Ms. Samuels."

Erin turned toward the voice and her eyes widened in surprise. The man was huge, big and brawny but with a friendly face and a wide smile. He reminded her of Yogi Bear.

"Mr. Mason?" she asked as she rose and extended her hand.

"The same," he said with a nod. His hand was like a bear's paw, swallowing hers whole. Then he released her and waved his hand. "Sit, sit. Make yourself comfortable."

Erin sank back into the chair and watched as he ambled around the desk and dropped into the leather chair. Now she understood why the desk was so massive. Mr. Mason would never have been able to fit behind anything smaller.

With his beefy hands he shuffled through the papers on his desk then he grabbed a sheet and held it up. "Here we are. Quite an impressive resume," he said and gave her a smile and a look that made him seem genuinely impressed. " Summa cum laude. Wow. You must be genius material."

Erin blushed, grateful for the compliment but a bit uncomfortable with his praise. "I study hard, that's all."

"And you know what that tells me about you?" Mike said, slamming the paper on the table. "You're a hard worker. You're the kind of person we want here. Now when can you start?"

"Wh…what? That's it? Aren't you going to ask me any questions?" Erin stared at the man, wondering if he'd gone mad. What kind of interview was this?

"Nope. I read your resume, now I've seen you, and I like you. That's it." He shrugged then leaned back in the chair and locked his fingers across his paunch. "So do you want the job or not?"

Erin knitted her brows in confusion. "I...do want the job." She gave him a bright smile. "I can start right away, Mr. Mason."

"Good. We have a party of twenty-two coming in this afternoon and that's in addition to our regular customers so it's going to be busy. Sally will get you a uniform and you'll be good to go." He pulled out a sheet of paper from a folder and slid it across the desk toward her. "Now let's talk money."

Erin didn't bother to hide her smile. She liked the sound of that. A lot.

Her luck had finally turned and now she could breathe again. She'd work hard and tuck away as much money as she could. She guessed she could hide her pregnancy for another three months, tops, and then, God help her, she'd be on her own. Mr. Mason seemed like a nice man but how would he react when he learned of her condition? She could only pray he'd be sympathetic.

But she had to prepare for the worst. As she signed the papers she thought of the tiny life growing inside her. 'Don't you worry, little one," she whispered silently. 'You and me, we'll make it together."

***

"Dare. Are you with me, man?"

Dare dragged his eyes back into focus and stared across his desk at the grinning man.

"You've been out of it lately," his long-time friend and business associate said with a laugh. "If I didn't know you I'd say you were in love."

Dare frowned at him but said nothing. The statement did not warrant an answer. Bart knew him. He had no time for women, least of all the money-hungry kind. There were always plenty of those around. He had his pick. The problem was, he wanted none of them. But there was one woman he could not get off his mind. A slender woman with chestnut hair that curled around her heart-shaped face, a woman with hazel eyes that flashed with the fire of her passion. Bart was right. There was something wrong with him. He was not in love but damn it, he was obsessed. He could not get

Erin out of his mind. "Sorry about that," Dare growled then pulled his chair close to the desk. "Let's get back to the business at hand."

"Cool." Bart ran his fingers through his spiky blonde hair then tilted the chair back until it looked dangerously close to tipping over. "It's a sweet deal. You can't pass up on this one. I got a tip on it. Going real cheap, considering."

"You're sure?" Dare admired his friend's ability to find great real estate deals. Bart found the deals and he financed them. That was how he'd acquired resorts on four other islands.

"Trust me, man. You can't lose out on this one." Bart leaned forward, his face earnest. "I can sniff out a deal a hundred miles away. You know I'm good at that."

He was. Dare could not deny it. Working together they'd become billionaires in the real estate business, buying up resorts in the Caribbean and condos in the United States and Canada then renovating and selling them for far more than they'd invested.

"This one's big though, Bart." Dare watched the other man intently. "My biggest investment yet."

"The one you're going to make the most money on," Bart responded.

"But I'm paying almost full price for this one."

"You can buy this resort 'as is'. You'll be filling it with guests in no time. Guaranteed."

"We'll see," Dare said. Then, against his will, his mind drifted to other things like the heat that coursed through him every time he thought of curly-haired Erin. It was no use. He couldn't concentrate. "Let's call it a day," he said and got up. "I've got some other business to take care of."

"Why is my mind telling me it's got something to do with a woman?" Bart was giving him that Cheshire Cat grin again.

"Go home, Bart." Dare walked over to the door and held it open. "This one's got nothing to do with you." He softened his statement with a brief smile.

"All right, my boy. But if you need any advice you know who to call."

It would be a dark day before Dare turned to Bart for advice on women. The man had married and divorced three times already. Still, he chuckled. "I'll bear that in mind."

After Bart left Dare walked over to the large bay window that looked out onto the ocean breaking against the shore. He crossed his arms and as he stared out onto the blue water his mind, as it had done so many times over the past few months, went back to Erin Samuels.

He'd pulled the hotel records and checked her out. Erin Samuels, student at Canucka College in Vancouver, Canada. Her home address was recorded as well as her cell phone number and e-mail address. For emergency contact she'd conspicuously left it blank. She probably didn't want her family being informed of her antics while on spring break. She could have any number of reasons. He'd seen guests leave out that portion before.

So he'd had all her information for the past three and a half months and he'd done absolutely nothing with it. Wimp. He grimaced as he berated himself inwardly. He wanted to see Erin Samuels again.

Dare gave a bitter laugh. He knew what she was but he'd held out long enough. He had to see her again, if even for the sole purpose of getting her out of his system. First order of business, he'd get his P.I. to check everything out, make sure she was still at the location in the file. Then he'd go there himself.

His mind made up, he went over to the desk and pressed the intercom.

"Yes, Mr. DeSouza." Cool and efficient, the voice of his personal assistant crackled through the speakers.

"Book me on a flight to Vancouver, please. I want to fly in day after tomorrow."

"Very well, Mr. DeSouza. Consider it done." Always discreet, Claudia didn't ask for any further details. She knew he would tell her all she needed to know.

Satisfied, Dare grabbed his keys and headed for the door. Erin Samuels was in for quite a surprise.

CHAPTER FIVE

Erin's first day on the job was a whirlwind of activity. The party of twenty-two showed up at one o'clock and after that there was a steady stream customers so that by the time the restaurant closed at ten o'clock that night she was worn to a near frazzle. How was she going to keep up with this pace, pregnant as she was?

She'd rejoiced at the job offer and she'd appreciated it. Really, she had. But what she hadn't anticipated was to be on her feet for twelve hours at a stretch with only two fifteen minute breaks and a half an hour for lunch.

That night when she got home, despite her best intentions, she was too tired to tackle step two in her plan - look for a cheaper apartment. She needed to move as soon as possible but her search would have to wait one more day.

Day two was almost as busy as the first. Benny's Restaurant was clearly a popular destination for all three meals of the day. From the moment Erin got to the restaurant she was kept running back and forth between the kitchen and the tables. Now she realized why 'Yogi Bear' as she'd come to think of him had hired her on the spot. She'd learned he'd lost a server the day before and clearly he had too much business to be short-staffed.

The work was tiring but her greatest consolation was the tips. She was almost collecting enough in tips as she would from her salary. Yet another perk of working at a restaurant and one she was so grateful for. She was saving every cent of it for the time when she'd need it most.

By nine o'clock that night the ache in Erin's feet turned to numbness and she kept glancing at the clock, willing it to speed up toward closing time. The crowd in the restaurant had thinned out with just a few diners lingering for dessert and coffee. Those, she could handle. With a sigh she was turning toward a high stool by the counter, intending to rest her feet for a minute, when a man, tall and dark-haired in a dark, immaculately tailored suit, walked in.

Erin frowned, feeling a twinge of recognition, and then her heart lurched as she recognized the man who filled the doorway. She could never forget those steel-gray eyes, eyes that now held her transfixed. It was Dare.

Suddenly feeling faint, Erin grabbed for the counter and held on. What was he doing here? He was from another time, another life. How in the world had he ended up at the very restaurant where she was working, thousands of miles from Santa Marta? He hadn't come looking for her, had he? He was walking toward her now, his eyes never leaving hers, and she stumbled back against the counter then froze. There was nowhere to run.

Why had he come? To insult her again? To throw her wantonness in her face? Her breath caught in her throat, her anxiety rising, knowing that his appearance could only mean trouble.

Dare was right in front of her now, looking down at her as if the two of them were the only people in the place.

"Erin Samuels. We meet again." His lips curled in a sardonic smile as he rested a hand on the counter beside her, trapping her into a corner.

"Dare, what are you doing here?" Her voice was little more than a strained whisper. She was fighting to regain her composure but his nearness, the earthy fragrance of his cologne, were overwhelming her senses. At that moment all she wanted to do was lean into him, feel his hard body against hers, have his arms wrapped around her. But it would not happen, it could not. Not when he despised her so much.

That thought ripped her out of her trance. Dare hated her. He'd used her then thrown her out of his bed. Now he'd strolled back into her life thinking she would do what? Swoon and throw herself at him again? He must be out of his mind. She glared up at him as he towered over her. "Excuse me but I have to get back to work." Her voice was as cool as the steel of his eyes. "I'm sure there is someone else who can assist you." If he thought she was going to serve him he'd better think again.

She stepped around him, intent on putting as much distance as possible between them.

His hand shot out, halting her flight. "Not so fast, honey. We need to talk. When you finish working I'll be waiting. Over there." He jerked his chin toward an empty booth by the window. Without another word he released her and walked away.

For a second Erin could only stare. The nerve of him. We need to talk? About what? Apart from one night of mind-blowing sex there was nothing that existed between them. Absolutely nothing for them to talk about. And then she remembered. The baby. How in the name of heaven had he found out about the baby? That had to be the reason why he'd suddenly stomped back into her life. And what was he planning to do about it?

She gasped as a thought flashed into her mind. Had he come to demand that she terminate her pregnancy?

Blindly, she stumbled into the kitchen and leaned against the counter to catch her breath.

"Hey, are you all right?" Mildred, the sous chef, approached her, a look of concern on her face. "You look like you're about to pass out."

"N…no. I'm fine," she whispered then sucked in a deep breath. *Come on, Erin. You're stronger than this.* She lifted her head and gave Mildred a smile. "It just got a bit too hot out there. I'm okay now. Are any trays ready?"

Mildred pointed to a tray laden with cups and a pot of coffee. "Table sixteen." She shook her head. "Thank God the day is almost over."

Those last thirty minutes of her workday were the hardest of her life. Out of the corner of her eye she could see Dare sitting in the far booth, a glass and a bottle of wine in front of him. She'd moved with feigned ease, serving the customers, chatting with them and laughing where appropriate. But she could feel Dare's eyes burning into her. As discreetly as she could she slipped a paper napkin into her hand and turned away to dab at the perspiration beading her brow. She would never let him see her sweat.

As it neared ten o'clock Erin sidled into the kitchen then headed for the changing room. Moving swiftly, she shed her uniform and donned her street clothes then grabbed her purse. Tonight she would not leave through the front door as she normally did. She almost giggled as she thought of Dare waiting patiently for her return. He'd have a long wait.

She bid her farewell and slipped out the back door that led into a dingy alleyway then she hurried up the path and out to the main road where she took off, walking at a brisk pace.

She heard the purr of an engine and looked up just in time to see an ink-black Mercedes Benz convertible pull up beside her.

"Get in." Dare was scowling at her and his tone brooked no argument.

"I…don't need a ride," she said, clutching her purse tightly to her chest. "I'm fine."

She was backing away when his voice, clipped and cold, stopped her. "Don't make me come get you. I'll lift you up and throw you in here if I have to."

Erin froze. Then she slowly approached the car. He would do it. She could see it in his eyes. This time, she knew, it was best to give in. With a sigh she pulled the door open and slipped into the passenger seat.

She hadn't even settled in before he took off down the road, making her whip around to stare at him. "Where are you taking me?" she demanded.

"Home."

"But…you don't even know where I live."

He didn't even bother to respond. That was all the answer she needed. He did know. Was he having her watched? Had he been spying on her ever since she'd returned to Canada? Erin's heart pounded at the thought. He knew she was pregnant. He knew where she lived. What else did he know about her? Did he know about her past, too?

That thought was sobering, so much so that it left her at a loss for words. She'd meant to blast him with her rage, demand an explanation, but she could not. She was too worried about how much he knew.

Within minutes Dare was pulling into the visitors' parking area in front of Erin's apartment building. He switched off the engine and turned toward her. "Let's go," he said. "We need to talk."

Erin did not even bother to object. Before he could move to get the door she climbed out of the car and marched toward the entrance. If he had to run to catch up with her then it would serve him right.

Unfortunately for her, he didn't need to. Within seconds his long strides had him by her side so that by the time she got to the entrance it was he who held the door open for her. They crossed the lobby then rode the elevator in silence. Deliberately, she kept her eyes averted, breathing slowly, trying her best to calm her nerves. It was not an easy task, not when she was so close she could breathe in the masculine fragrance of his cologne. There was no way on earth she could ignore the fact that he was there, mere inches away from her. The shallowness of her breathing, the tautness of her nipples in her bra, were evidence of the effect he was having on her.

As soon as the elevator door opened Erin was out and away, eager to put distance between them. Her physical attraction was too strong, too disturbing. She had to regain control.

When he strode up behind her she was still at the door fiddling with her keys, her palms slippery with perspiration.

Calmly he reached out and plucked them from her hand, selected the correct one and opened the door. Then with a mocking smile he dropped the keys back into her hand. When they stepped inside the apartment a wave of embarrassment swept over her. Dare was obviously a man of wealth. He'd said something about being a billionaire. She seriously doubted that but she was sure he had some money. He carried himself like a man of means. What would he think of her home, so sparsely furnished that the living room didn't even have a sofa? She'd been meaning to get one since moving in but that had been almost two years ago. Now, under the present circumstances, the chances of acquiring that piece of furniture were slim to nil.

At least she had the essentials - a bed to sleep on and a chest of drawers for her few pieces of clothing. And at least she could offer him a seat. In the living room cum dining room were a small table and two chairs. It wouldn't make for comfortable sitting but maybe that was a good thing. Making him comfortable was the last thing she wanted to do. She wanted him to state his business then get the heck out of her apartment and her life.

Erin could feel her anger return. After Dare had used her and discarded her in the most horrible way, what could he possible want with her now?

Except for the baby, her heart whispered. Apart from the baby there was absolutely no reason why this man would have the slightest interest in her. This was all about the baby.

Erin waved a hand toward the table. "Have a seat. Please."

She could see that he was scrutinizing her home, his eyes roaming the apartment. She could just imagine what was going through his mind. All she needed to see was the expression on his face to know what he was thinking. She wasn't important enough for him. Now he was getting confirmation that he'd made the right decision in throwing her out.

Dare walked over, his height making her apartment seem too small and the ceiling too low. She was glad when he dropped his tall frame onto the chair. Seated, he was a little less intimidating. Just a little.

"Aren't you going to sit?" Dare was looking at her as she stood several feet away, watching him. On his face was an amused smile.

What was there to smile about? "No, I'm fine," she said and released the hand she'd just realized she'd been wringing in agitation. She tucked her hands into the pockets of her skirt. "Dare, what are you doing here? And how did you find me?"

He crossed his legs and leaned back in the chair, somehow managing to look comfortable. "Finding you was easy, honey. We've got all your details at the hotel."

"At the hotel?" Erin's eyes widened in shock. "They let you see my personal information? Who did you bribe?" She couldn't believe the breach to her personal privacy. Sunsational Resort would be getting a letter from her and it would not be pretty.

"Come off it, Erin. Stop playing dumb. It's not becoming." He gave a snort and crossed his arms over his chest. Gone was the look of relaxation. Now he looked exasperated. "Why would I need to bribe my own employees?"

"Your...employees?" What the heck was he talking about? Erin shook her head. The man was making no sense at all. "What employees?" Then, like a light bulb that had just been switched on something in her mind clicked. "You weren't a guest at the resort, were you? You actually work there."

How could she have been so stupid? The man was probably one of the managers at the resort. Now she understood why his villa had looked so grand in comparison to all the others. The man was a big shot at his workplace.

The realization made her all the more angry. "Do you realize I could have you fired?" Her voice was strong now as she realized the power she had over this man. He was an employee of the resort and yet he'd gotten involved with her, a guest, and then he'd had the audacity to show up at her workplace. And now he was in her home.

Now it was her turn to fold her arms across her chest. "You'd better have a darn good reason for being here or else you're going to be in a lot of trouble." Feeling smug at having the upper hand she gave him a smile but it was not a pleasant one. "What would your boss say if I told him that you'd slept with one of the guests? If I complain to your superiors you won't be in your cushy job for long."

Dare's eyes narrowed. Slowly, deliberately, he got up and then he was towering over her. "Are you threatening me?" His voice was hard as the granite of the countertop.

Erin took an involuntary step back. Had she gone too far? She was alone in the apartment with a man who looked just about ready to wring her neck. Goodness, she'd been so stupid. Why hadn't she kept her mouth shut?

"N…no," she managed to whisper. "It wasn't a threat."

A strange look passed over Dare's face and then the anger was gone. His look was almost one of regret. "Look, I'm sorry," he said and expelled his breath. "I didn't mean to scare you. You just annoyed the hell out of me with your pretense."

What pretense, she wanted to ask. Instead, she bit her lip and waited. There was no way she was going to incite his wrath again, not while she was still alone with him. She'd just let him have his say.

"You know I own Sunsational Resort so all this talk about my boss and getting me fired is a waste of my time and yours. Let's just be adults here and-"

"What did you say?" Erin's heart jerked in shock. "You own Sunsational Resort? Are you serious?"

Dare gave her an irritated look then he shook his head. "Here we go again. Will you stop pretending?"

"I'm not pretending," she retorted. "I had no idea you were…are… the owner of the resort."

His eyes narrowed. "You had no idea? So you're telling me that when you spent the night with me you didn't know who I was?"

Eyes wide, Erin shook her head. Now that he'd said it out loud it didn't sound good at all. Sleeping with a total stranger? She cringed inside just thinking about it. How could she blame him for having a low opinion of her?

She could feel the heat of shame rush to her face. He would never respect a woman like her. How could he? She had absolutely no excuse except for the fact that the night he'd taken her to his villa Dare had so captivated her that she hadn't found the power to resist him.

Mortified, Erin could only stare up at Dare and what she saw in his eyes made her wince. Was it scorn or disgust that registered there? Either way Erin knew she was lower than dirt in his eyes.

"Why should I believe you," he grated, "when you all but threw yourself into my arms? Twice. Why would you have done that if you didn't know who I was?"

"I don't need to explain myself," she said with far more bravado than she felt. "You wouldn't believe me, anyway."

"Try me."

She opened her mouth to object but then she breathed a sigh. What was the use? She might as well lay all her cards on the table and then he could do what he wished. "The first time I was just going to ask you out…as a dare, to satisfy my friends. I slipped and that was when I grabbed on to you."

"You weren't trying to kiss me?'

"Absolutely not."

"It sure looked like it."

"Well, I wasn't," she said, glaring at him. He didn't have to look so pleased with the idea. "And the second time, in the bar, it was pure coincidence that I bumped into you. I was trying to get away from a most annoying man and saw you as my means of escape."

"Oh, so that's all I was to you."

"That's all."

"And the third time?"

"What third time?"

"Your going out on the date with me, then to the villa. What's your excuse for that one?"

"I…" She swallowed. She had no idea how to explain that one away. Finally, she said, "You were the one who invited me."

For a long time he stared at her then he spoke, his look enigmatic. "So it was." He nodded slowly. "So it was."

Now what did that mean? Did he believe her or was she still nothing more than a groupie in his eyes?

Well, groupie or not, Dare was here in her apartment, thousands of miles from his resort and his island, and she needed to know why. He'd certainly not come all this way out of love for her.

She was loath to broach the subject but since he seemed intent on skirting around the real reason for his visit Erin decided to take the plunge. She'd always faced her problems head on and she wasn't going to stop now, even if it meant facing off with the lion in her apartment.

"Dare, I've asked you twice and you've not given me an answer. Why are you here?" She lifted her chin and looked him squarely in the eyes. "Is it because of the baby? You want to state your claim?"

Erin never saw someone's expression change so fast. His frown disappeared. In his eyes was a look of shock that was like a slap to her face. He hadn't known. Dare had not had any inkling that she was expecting his child.

"Baby? Are you…pregnant?"

Erin bit her lip and dropped her eyes. Goodness, she'd said quite enough already. Oh, Lord. She'd let the proverbial cat out of the bag and now she would have to face the consequences.

"Erin, are you pregnant?" This time his voice was stern but the shock was replaced by a calm that almost seemed more dangerous. "Tell me."

She swallowed but still she could not speak. Neither could she look in his eyes. She did not want to see the condemnation there. This was her baby, and no matter what she would not feel shame for carrying this life inside of her.

In the end, she just nodded.

He expelled his breath. "And the baby is mine?"

Erin's eyes flew to his and her mouth fell open in shocked anger. "Of course it's yours. What? Do you think I make it a habit of going around sleeping with different men?"

"How should I know?" His retort was quick and brutal. "You fell into bed with me easily enough."

"Do you know what? Just leave my apartment. Get out before I call the police. I don't need to stand here taking your insults." She marched over to the door and flung it open. "Leave. Now."

Dare gave her a lethal look then strode toward her. As she stepped back he gripped the door and slammed it shut.

Erin gasped. Who did he think he was? "What are you doing? You'd better go."

"Listen to me," he said through clenched teeth, "you can't drop that bombshell and then expect me to walk away simply because you tell me to. I need to know. Are you expecting my child?"

"Yes, Dare, I'm expecting your child as I think you already know." She practically spat the words at him. "But never fear. I don't expect a thing from you. I've already made arrangements for the baby so don't feel you have to contribute anything. And," her voice rose and she pointed an accusing finger at him, "if you came all this way to try to convince me to get rid of my child you can just turn around and go right back to Santa Marta because it's not going to happen."

"Get rid of…what the hell?" Dare raised his hand and she flinched but he simply raked his fingers through his hand. There was a look of confusion on his face. "I don't understand. I used protection every time."

Seeing his bewildered state Erin softened just a little. "They're not one hundred percent guaranteed. You should know that."

"Yeah, I do, but I thought they'd have been good enough for one night." He shook his head. "And you're not on the pill?"

"No."

"But what are the odds…" he began then his voice trailed off and his eyes took on a faraway look as if he was trying to remember something. Then a look of realization crossed his face. "It must have been that third time. When you left and I rolled over there was some dampness on the bed but I didn't think anything of it. The condom must have broken."

"But you would have seen that."

"If it was a small tear, probably not. I don't sit there inspecting the damn things. Once I'm done I just get rid of them."

For a moment there was silence as they both fell into deep thought. Erin had no idea what was going through Dare's mind but her dilemma was coming to terms with the fact that he hadn't known about the baby and yet he was here. What was the explanation for that? Dared she ask?

She sucked in a deep breath. She had to know. Steeling herself against his anger she blurted, "So if you didn't come about the baby why are you here?"

"What?" Dare looked like she'd just pulled him out of a trance.

"Why are you here, Dare? Why did you come looking for me?"

His eyes honed in on hers and for the first time since she'd met him he seemed at a loss for words.

Then his face darkened in a scowl. "I came to take you back to Santa Marta."

CHAPTER SIX

"To take me back?" she spluttered, a look of incredulity on her face. "Are you mad?"

"I'm quite sane, I can assure you," he said, the pace of his heart returning to normal. The girl had turned the tables on him and given him the shock of his life.

"But…why?"

Dare almost felt sorry for her, she looked so confused. He knew he must be driving her round the bend but how could he help that? He couldn't explain it even to himself. One day he'd seen her then spent the following night making sweet love to her and, like the fish in the sea, he was hooked. The funny thing was it seemed Erin hadn't even realized she'd caught the biggest fish in the pond.

"Why, Dare? You threw me out of your bed, remember? Out of your life. So what's this story about coming back to get me?" She threw her hands up in apparent frustration. "For what? Another one night stand?"

She was glaring at him now, her chest heaving with the intensity of her emotions. And who could blame her?

He'd done everything she'd accused him of, and more. Little did she know that he'd seduced her expertly and deliberately into going back to his villa and making love to him. He'd wanted to make her pay for pursuing him so shamelessly. He'd wanted to take what she was offering. And now he would pay the steepest price. His days of philandering were over. He was about to become a father.

He still could not believe it. Dare DeSouza, family man. When he'd left Santa Marta he'd had no idea that the joke would be on him.

But in the end it could all turn out in his favor. Obsessed with the memory of Erin he'd finally given in and come to see her with the intention of convincing her to return to the island. Now, with this development, there was no way she could say no.

"Erin, calm down. Have a seat." He walked over and pulled out a chair. When she hesitated he frowned. "Come and sit before you keel over."

Thankfully, she headed over on shaky legs and sank down on the chair. If she hadn't he would have gone over and lifted her off her feet. He could see that her emotions coupled with her tiredness from work were beginning to take its toll. She was shaking.

He walked into the kitchen and filled a glass with water then brought it to her.

She gulped it thirstily then rested the glass on the table and looked up at him.

It was only then, in the light cast by the chandelier above the table, that he saw how thin and drawn she was. Her eyes were large molten pools in her face. They were circled with shadows of exhaustion.

He pulled the other chair forward and sat beside her. "Erin," he said, drawing her eyes back to his face, "you look terrible."

She looked surprised at his outspokenness then her face broke into a tired smile. "Thanks. You are so kind."

"I mean it," he said, his voice low and grave. "You need to stop this work you're doing. It's too much."

At that she laughed but there was no mirth to the sound. "Stop this work, he says. And then eat what? Air? And how would I pay my rent and my bills?"

"I have the solution for that," he said. "I want you to-"

"Oh yes, come back to Santa Marta," she said, her tone sarcastic. "You forgot. When you came here you expected to take a slender, sexy thing back with you. I'm not any of that. Not anymore."

"Erin," Dare said, trying to keep his voice calm, "listen to me. I want you-"

"No, you don't," she snapped. "Not anymore. Not when I'm going to look like a pumpkin in three-"

Dare had reached his limit. "Woman, will you be quiet and let me speak?" he bellowed. "I want you to marry me."

Erin recoiled as if he'd slapped her. Then her face flushed red and her eyes flashed. "I don't appreciate you laughing at me, Dare. If this is all a joke to you I think you'd better leave."

"It's not a joke," he said quietly. "I'm serious. I want you as my wife."

"But…why?" Her voice was a mere whisper and she looked back at him with huge eyes.

"I would think that's quite obvious. You're the mother of my child."

"Not yet, I'm not."

"Oh, but you are. The youngest of the DeSouza line is now growing inside you."

"DeSouza." She said the name, a look of wonder on her face. "Can you believe I never even knew your last name?" Her cheeks grew red and she dropped her eyes as if in shame.

"There's no need to feel bad, Erin. Just forget the past and look toward the future as my wife."

"As your wife." She repeated the words but there was no enthusiasm there. Then she looked over at him. "You never even asked me the question."

"Of course I did."

"No, you said you want me to marry you. You never asked me." Her mouth was set in a cute pout.

Dare laughed. If a question was what she wanted then a question she would get. He would not be accused of not being romantic.

Just to make it more touching and more likely to be in keeping with her romantic notions Dare slid off the chair and went down on one knee. He took her slim hand in his then looked deep into her eyes. "Erin Samuels," he said, his voice firm and full of meaning, "will you marry me?" Then he lifted her hand to his lips and kissed the back of it.

For a moment she only stared at him then her hazel eyes flashed and she snatched her hand from his grasp. "No," she said, her voice vehement and hard. "Never in a million years."

What the hell? Taken aback, Dare remained on his knees. Then, never taking his eyes off her flushed face he rose to his feet. Only then did he speak. "What the blazes was that all about?"

She lifted her face and gave him a look of defiance. "I said I'd never marry you."

"Then why did you make me ask you?" He could feel the anger rise in him. Did she think she was playing with a damn puppy?

"I wanted you to ask me so I could give you my answer," she said, her tone smug. "And the answer is no."

"Why?"

She gave a toss of her head and one of her brown curls fell across her face. She lifted a delicate hand and brushed it away. "You rejected me so now it's my turn to reject you."

"Oh, being petty are we? So you would reject my offer knowing that you can't support yourself and the child. You would do this just to prove a point."

"I can support my baby and me." She had the audacity to look offended. "We don't need you."

He folded his arms across his chest and glared down at her. "If you think I'm going to let you raise my child in this dump you're out of your mind."

"Dump? You're calling my home a dump?"

"Forgive me. Your humble abode." His voice dripped with sarcasm. "My child will not be living here nor growing up here. My child will be with me in Santa Marta."

She gave a harsh laugh. "I want to see how you're going to accomplish that when I'm not going anywhere."

"You are."

"I'm not."

Dare could feel his nostrils flare in annoyance. Not a good sign. Erin was intent on pushing him to breaking point. He was going to end this before things went too far.

"Now you listen to me. You will come back to Santa Marta with me and you will marry me. If you don't then be prepared to be cut off from the child altogether."

"What do you mean, cut off from the child? You can't do that." Her voice had risen and he heard the fear registered there.

He pressed home his advantage. "Oh, can't I? There's something to be said about having money, Erin. With money comes power. I have a lot of it and you don't."

Erin stared up at him, eyes wide and uncertain. He could see that she was vulnerable now.

"I can hire the best lawyers to present a case that it would be in the best interest of the child to be with me. I can provide everything that he or she would need unlike you who can barely manage to sustain yourself."

She was pale now, and silent. His words were having the impact he'd intended. He decided to drive another nail into the coffin. "There's a good chance you'll lose custody, Erin. Do you want to take that risk?"

"You…wouldn't." Her voice was a broken whisper.

"I would." He would not yield. Not now. He was too close to victory. "Marry me, Erin, and all your problems will be solved. You won't have to worry about money, the care of the baby, anything. But if you choose the other path, know that I will do everything in my power to claim my heir."

For a long time Erin did not respond. Then her lower lip began to tremble and she turned her face away. "You're such a bastard," she said with a sob and covered her face with her hands.

Dare said nothing. He might be a bastard but he was a bastard determined to get what he wanted. He'd come all this way to get Erin Samuels and he was not going home without her.

He could see she was defeated. He softened his stance and went over to take her in his arms, comfort her and let her see she was in good hands.

As soon as his hand touched her shoulder she wrenched away and when she looked up at him her eyes spat fire. "Don't touch me," she said through clenched teeth. "I may have to marry you but I will never be your wife."

Dare sucked in his breath and scowled. So that was the way it was, was it? A marriage in name only.

Well, he'd already won the first battle. She would marry him. Once he got her back to the island he would take on this second hurdle. He was looking forward to the challenge. He smiled to himself. There were ways to make a woman yield and he was an expert at every one of them.

"Get some rest," he said calmly. "I'll be back in the morning to work out the details. Let your boss know you won't be coming back."

He didn't bother to wait for a reply. He knew she was numb from shock and exhaustion. He let himself out of the apartment and headed for the elevator where he gave a satisfied sigh. Erin Samuels was his at last.

***

Within a week of Dare's arrival Erin was in a private jet on the way back to the island of Santa Marta but this time as the wife of one of the richest and most powerful men in that land. So why wasn't she over the moon with joy?

Instead, she felt sick inside. Had she sold her soul to this devil, Dare DeSouza? He'd given her an ultimatum and she'd cracked under the pressure, scared out of her mind that he would follow through on his threat. He could be a ruthless man. She had no doubt about that and she wasn't taking any chances where her child was concerned.

A limousine met them at the airport and they traveled in silence, Erin flipping through a magazine or at least pretending to, and Dare engrossed in whatever it was he was reading on his iPad.

About twenty minutes into their journey the limousine turned off the main road and drove through the stately gates of what looked like a resort. As Erin glanced up she frowned. This was not how she remembered the entrance to Sunsational Resort. She sat up and looked out the window. They were traveling up a palm-lined driveway that climbed a gentle hill and then the limousine turned and there she saw on the crest of the hill a majestic mansion that made her eyes widen. Huge palms graced its courtyard and framed the gleaming ivory walls and red and gold flowers were sprinkled amongst the rich green leaves that formed a soft carpet along its base. It had the look of an opulent tropical paradise.

Was this Dare's home? Erin stole a quick glance at him and saw that he was watching her with hooded eyes. She turned away again. If he'd hoped to impress her he'd certainly done that, and more. She couldn't imagine living in a place like this. The resort had been luxury enough.

The chauffeur slowed the car to a halt then came around to hold the door open for them. As he helped her out of the car Erin continued to stare, admittedly overwhelmed by the grandeur before her.

Then Dare was by her side. He took her hand in his and led her up the steps and into his lavish home. As they passed the threshold they heard the sound of hurried footsteps then a tiny woman with her hair pulled into a bun entered the foyer.

"Welcome, welcome Mrs. DeSouza. We've been expecting you." Her eyes crinkled in a smile so bright Erin had to respond with a smile of her own. The woman had called her Mrs. DeSouza. It had sounded strange to her ears but that was who she was now - the mistress of the house. Sort of. She had to remind herself not to get carried away. Dare had brought her here under duress. This was anything but a fairy-tale marriage.

"Erin, this is Francine Lopez," Dare said with a warm smile that was both surprising and refreshing. It was obvious that he had genuine regard for the woman. "She's my right hand."

"Oh, Senor Dare, you are too kind." The woman smiled back at him then she turned her full attention to Erin. "I am the housekeeper. I have run this house for Senor Dare for the past four years but now that you are here, senora, you will give the orders."

That brought a smile to Erin's face. "I don't think so," she said with a little laugh.

"Oh, yes." The housekeeper nodded emphatically. "The woman, she is in charge of the house. The man, he knows nothing about the house, only about making money."

"Hey," Dare objected with an exaggerated frown. "Are you saying all these years I thought I was in charge I really wasn't?"

"That is so, Senor Dare. That is why you have me."

There was a twinkle in Francine's eyes that bore testament to the comfort she felt with her employer. Apparently Dare had a pleasant side, one that he reserved for a select few.

"Now come, let me take you upstairs to your suite. You must be tired after your journey." The housekeeper waved her hand and ushered her toward a wide, winding staircase.

Her suite? From the look of the house Erin could just imagine what that looked like. Could she survive more luxury in one day? But she had to admit, she'd loved the sound of the word, not because of the affluence it denoted but because it sounded like she'd be far removed from Dare DeSouza. Of course, he would have a suite of his own.

She glanced back at him and saw that he was still standing there, his gray eyes unreadable as he watched her climb the staircase. She hastened to turn her attention back to Francine and her friendly chatter.

She was now in the lion's den. And she would best be prepared to face what was to come. She would seek refuge in this suite of hers and there she would rest up and then plot her next course of action. At the top of the list would be strategies to stay out of Dare's way. Little did he know it but the man, dastardly though he was, still held a place in her heart. And that, more than anything, made him the most dangerous of foes.

***

Erin was grateful to find that the trials of her pregnancy seemed to be behind her. There were no more bouts of morning sickness, no dizzy spells, and her appetite had returned with a vengeance. She'd been on the island five days now and she and Francine had developed an automatic friendship that surprised her.

She learned that Francine Lopez was in her fifties, the mother of three grown sons who had all left the island for jobs in North America. One was an engineer working in Alaska for a major oil company, another was a professor at a community college in New Jersey, and the third had opened a business in Florida, a chain of dollar-concept stores. They all had families of their own and were doing well and Francine could not have been more proud.

Francine did admit, though, that at times she got lonely and wished that even one of them had remained on the island so that she could have her grandchildren around her. Visits to the United States a few times per year were just not enough. She was glad to have gotten this job with Senor DeSouza because she now came to see him almost as her own son. But she had been hinting - subtly, of course, because he was still her employer and it was not her place - that he might want to consider settling down and starting a family. Secretly she'd harbored the dream of seeing the house full of little ones. What a joy that would be. And now, as she'd told Erin, he had finally made the big step and brought home a wife. Now the house would be filled with the laughter of children.

Erin only smiled at Francine words. If only she knew how close she was to her dream. Well, she would know soon enough. A pregnancy was not something you could hide for long.

Today again, Erin was enjoying Francine's company as she sat at the wrought iron table on the cobbled patio that looked out onto a kidney-shaped pool.

"You used sunscreen today, yes?" The older woman's face showed a hint of concern. "The sun, it is very strong today and your skin looks delicate. You must protect yourself."

Erin chuckled. "Si, mama," she teased and rolled her eyes cheekily. She was having fun with Francine's over protectiveness. The housekeeper was like a fussy mother hen, always making sure she was comfortable and always admonishing her to take care. Erin could only imagine how this mothering would escalate once she learned her condition.

Francine looked as pleased as a kitty with a saucer of milk when she heard Erin's reply. Maybe it was some consolation to her that she now had someone to fuss over.

And Erin did not mind one bit. In fact, Francine was now like the mother she no longer had. She remembered when the older lady asked about her family back in Canada.

"I don't have any," she replied and her breath caught in her throat. It had been nine years but the memory of the tragedy was still raw and painful.

"No family?" Francine asked, her tone incredulous. "How is that?"

"I am…was an only child. My parents were both killed in a car accident when I was twelve."

Francine gasped then her face softened in sympathy. "Oh, nina, how terrible."

"Yes," Erin said with a sigh. "It was hard. It still is. But you deal with what life gives you. What else can you do?"

"And how did you survive without your parents?"

"Foster care." She kept her voice neutral, trying to keep the bitterness from her tone. For her, the experiences had not been pleasant.

"I ended up moving from family to family, each one worse than the one before." She smiled at Francine through misty eyes. "I was relieved when I turned eighteen and could move out and live on my own terms."

"Ah, nina," Francine crooned, "life can be very cruel. *Gracias a dios*, you are here now and you are safe with Senor Dare."

Erin almost laughed at that. Safe with Dare? She doubted it.

So far he had left her to her own devices which was exactly what she wanted. Apparently there'd been some developments with his business which were keeping him busy. Whatever it was, she hoped it would continue for a long time. She could do without his attention. She'd told him she'd wanted the marriage to be in name only and she meant it.

Her ringing cell phone broke into her thoughts. "Excuse me." She hopped up and dashed into the sunroom where she'd left the phone. It was unusual for her cell phone to ring. Since leaving college she hadn't maintained contact with any of her former college mates. She was wondering who it could be when she picked it up and peered at the screen. Robyn O'Riley. Erin's heart sank. If Robyn was calling it could not be good.

She clicked on the answer button and put the phone to her ear. "Hello."

"Erin, you naughty girl, how could you do this to me?" Robyn's words were teasing but her tone gave her away. She was annoyed.

"Do what?" Erin rolled her eyes. Robyn was famous for putting on an act. She was always the wounded woman.

"Don't play with me," Robyn said, the pretense falling and her voice harsh. "You went and got married and didn't even tell me."

Erin stiffened. How in the world had Robyn found out? She had told absolutely no-one.

"You made me have to read about it in the tabloids. How could you?"

The tabloids? Erin's heart sank. So much for keeping all of this a secret. And why hadn't she thought about the possibility of something like that happening?

Dare was a rich man and an eligible bachelor. The paparazzi must have jumped at the chance to break the news of his change in status. Somehow, though, because his business was all the way in Santa Marta she hadn't expected the publicity.

"I almost missed it," Robyn was saying, her tone growing increasingly irritated. "It was a small feature tucked in the corner of the second page. If I hadn't caught sight of it I would never have known. You weren't going to tell me, were you?"

"I…" Erin bit her lip. She hated to lie. It was the truth. She'd had absolutely no intention of telling Robyn anything.

"Still keeping secrets, Erin?" Robyn's voice was low and threatening. Her true nature was showing through. "You know I'm the last person you should keep a secret from."

Erin remained silent. The last thing she wanted was get on Robyn's wrong side. She knew too much and was more than ready to use her knowledge to her own advantage.

"Why didn't you tell me the guy you'd been seeing over spring break was the owner of the resort?" she demanded.

"I had no idea-"

"Do you expect me to believe that? You knew who he was and that was why you spent the night." Robyn's voice was hard with accusation.

Erin knew exactly what her problem was. Robyn should have been the one to snap up the most eligible bachelor on the island, not some poor church mouse of a girl like her. Robyn's parents had money. Not within Dare's range by any means, but she was used to enjoying the trappings of wealth and would have loved the chance to secure an even more prosperous future through marriage with a man like Dare.

It was no use arguing with her, not when her mind was all made up. The best thing would be for this conversation to end without Robyn's feathers being ruffled even more than they already were. Erin decided to change the subject. "How are your parents?"

"Dad's fine." Robyn's response was curt. For some reason, Robyn didn't mention her mother. She was probably on one of her long trips to South America.

"I'm glad to hear your dad's well." Erin didn't have a whole lot more to say to Robyn after that. After all, what would she have to say to the girl who had tormented her for the five months she'd spent in her home under foster care? "I'm glad to hear it."

Mr. and Mrs. O'Riley had been distant but kind, providing more than adequately for her needs while she was under their roof. The first time she met them, when she'd been the insecure age of seventeen, she'd immediately recognized them as people of high social standing. For the life of her she could not figure out why they'd chosen to get involved with foster care. It was not until she'd been there a month that Erin found out that the year before they'd done a tour with a missionary group and had felt obligated to do their part in the community. And so they'd taken her in.

Little did they know that they had a devil among them. Of their three children Robyn was the oldest and bossiest. What made it worse, she was deceitful. Things had started out manageable even though Robyn seemed to think that with the new arrival she'd suddenly acquired a personal servant. Not wanting to put her position in jeopardy, Erin acquiesced most of the time and with each 'favor' she did for Robyn the girl mellowed to her.

Then came the night when, overcome with loneliness and depression, Erin crept into the bathroom to weep in private. That was where Robyn found her, curled up on the bathroom floor, her face buried in a thick bathrobe in an attempt to stifle her sobs.

In that moment of weakness she had shared a secret with Robyn. That was a big mistake. Thereafter the girl used that knowledge to her advantage.

And now she was doing it again. Erin had no idea what Robyn was up to but it could not be good. It never was.

"I'm coming back to Santa Marta. To visit you."

"Excuse me?"

"I want to come for a visit," Robyn said, even more emphatically this time. "We haven't spoken in a while. We need to do some catching up."

The only catching up Robyn wanted to do was to get to know the billionaire ex-bachelor Erin had 'stolen' from under her nose. That was exactly what she was thinking. Erin had no doubt about that.

But Robyn knew too much. And if she felt it would serve her purpose she'd be all too ready to spill those precious beans.

Erin had to think fast. How could she keep Robyn from coming to the island?

"I'm not sure this is a good time."

"Baloney. Now is a great time. I've got to come see you before you get bogged down with marriage. Now let's see…" There was the sound of paper flipping and then Robyn spoke again. "I'm free all of next week. I'll come in on Sunday. I'll e-mail you my flight information so you can pick me up at the airport."

"Robyn, I don't think you should book any flights just yet." Erin's voice was firm. "I need to discuss this with Dare. What if he's not ready for visitors?"

"Nonsense. A girl needs to have her friends around her especially at this sensitive time when she's adjusting to a new life. I have no doubt that you can convince him of that." There was hardness in her tone and Erin knew immediately. Robyn was issuing a not-so-subtle threat.

So that was how it was. Either give in to Robyn's 'self-invitation' or risk the negative repercussions.

She could not take that risk.

Erin sighed. "Okay, I'll speak to him tonight but please don't book any flights till I get back to you."

After Erin hung up she sat for a moment deep in thought. This was not good. She did not like either one of her options. If she tried to keep Robyn away the girl would stir up trouble for sure. And if she came to the island and, even worse, came to stay at the house, Robyn would find some way to make her life miserable. That was Robyn.

Erin drew a deep breath then stood up. She would talk to Dare and then she would start planning. She would have to keep Robyn as busy as possible so she would have no opportunity to be alone with Dare. There was no telling what Robyn would let slip. Erin could see it already. The coming week was going to be a nightmare.

CHAPTER SEVEN

"I don't like it, Dare." Roger's voice was grave. "I don't like it one bit."

At those words Dare's sense of foreboding mushroomed into dread. Roger had been his accountant for over ten years and even when he'd undertaken the riskiest business deals not once had the man expressed such doubt.

But this time was different.

"How bad is it?" Dare almost didn't want to ask but he had to know. He'd never been one to back away from his problems.

"This is your biggest investment so far."

Dare nodded. "Over two hundred and fifty million."

Roger pursed his lips. "I hate to say this, Dare, but it may also be your worst."

The statement was almost a physical blow to Dare. He shoved his chair back and got up. He began to pace the room. Then he stopped and looked over at Roger who was still staring at him, his face morose.

"I don't understand," Dare said with a shake of his head. "Bart told me this was the best deal yet. He's never been wrong before."

"Even so, you should have sent in the experts to check out the property."

"We did. Bart and I discussed it and he made all the arrangements."

"Did he?" Roger's voice was quiet but the look he gave Dare was pointed.

For a moment Dare stared back at him in silence then he raked his fingers through his hair. "I think he did," he said with a heavy sigh. "I hope to God he did."

Roger shook his head. "Couldn't have. Any of the experts could have told you the structures are faulty and irreparable. Any of them could have prevented this. That's what they're there for-"

"All right, I get the point." Dare shoved his hands into his pockets. "I screwed up."

Roger said nothing. He dropped his eyes to peer at the figures on the paper in his hand. Then he looked up. "Did you even see the place?"

"Of course I did. I wouldn't have bought it sight unseen."

"And you didn't see anything to indicate the place was a wreck?"

Dare shrugged. "It looked fine to me. Nothing that some paint wouldn't have put right. Of course, I was relying on professional feedback and that is what I thought I got with those reports."

Roger sighed. "When were you planning on opening this resort?"

"Seeing that all the buildings were in place I was aiming for a Christmas launch. The agency has already started working on the advertising campaign."

"Call it off," Roger said bluntly. "Unless some kind of miracle happens there's no way you'll be ready for a Christmas launch. That's just six months away and the way things look you're going to have to knock down half of those villas and rebuild. A strong gust of wind would knock the damn things off their foundation."

Dare nodded slowly but his mind was miles away. He was thinking about the one man he'd thought he could trust with his life. He'd known Bart Reynolds since college when they'd been roommates and they'd both pursued degrees in engineering. Even while still studying they'd dreamed big dreams and immediately upon graduation they had executed all they'd discussed throughout their junior and senior years. Together they'd found phenomenal success and made a place for themselves among the wealthiest people in the world.

Bart had been there with him every step of the way. So what the hell happened?

Dare raised his head and looked Roger in the eyes. "I'm going to get to the bottom of this and when I do somebody is going to pay."

***

Dare didn't get home till about ten o'clock that night. Even though she was dying to slide into her bed Erin stayed up until she heard the low purr of his car coming up the driveway.

As she heard the front door open she got up from the sofa and pulled the robe tightly around her then tied the sash. She was not cold. She'd deliberately dressed in long pajamas so she was covered from neck to ankles. Feet, if you counted the fuzzy slippers she was wearing. She was making it absolutely clear that she was making no advances.

The door slammed and she heard Dare's footsteps as he began to walk across the foyer and toward his suite. She hurried to catch him before he disappeared.

"Dare," she said, her voice echoing in the dimly lit hallway. He froze then slowly turned to look at her. He'd slipped his jacket off his shoulders and was holding it loosely in one hand. He was in white shirt-sleeves rolled back from his wrists and his tie hung loose around his neck. His face was hidden in shadows so there was no way to determine his expression.

Still, she assumed he was tired so she spoke in a gentle, unassuming voice. "May I talk to you for a minute?"

She was totally unprepared for his response.

"What now?" He snarled then stepped into the light.

And that was when she saw his face - dark and frowning and strained. He'd obviously had a rough day.

"I'm sorry," she said quickly. "It looks like this is a bad time."

He looked annoyed. "You already stopped me so go ahead."

"No, it's fine," she insisted. "It can wait until tomorrow."

"Spill it, Erin. I don't have time for games. You wanted to talk, so talk."

She took a small step back, shocked at his vehemence. What had she done to deserve his anger? And what right did he have to speak to her like that?

"No," she said, her tone firm. "I will not have any discussion with you if that's the attitude you're going to take. We will have this talk tomorrow." Did he feel he was the only one who could have an attitude? He would learn soon enough that she could be just as stubborn as he.

Dare sucked in his breath then let it out in a sigh that told of a world of troubles. "Listen, I'm sorry I barked at you. It's been a long day." He threw his jacket onto a nearby table. "Let's go to the kitchen. I need a drink."

He led the way, his long strides eating up the yards to the kitchen. She padded along behind, discreetly admiring the curve of his muscled shoulders, his narrow waist and a butt that looked delicious in his tailored trousers.

The look of him brought back memories of that night so many months ago, that precious night when she had felt like liquid velvet in his arms. She'd had no power to resist him. And - most horrifying of all - she'd fancied herself to be falling in love with him. She shook her head, clearing that idea fast. If she knew what was good for her she'd get her mind back to earth. The man did not want her. That was clear.

In the kitchen Dare poured himself a drink while Erin pulled out a chair and sat down. He put the glass to his lips and drained it in one gulp then he took a deep breath and walked over to drop his long frame in the chair across from Erin. He cocked an eyebrow. "So what's the problem?"

"I didn't say there was a problem," Erin said and gave him a smile to soften her words. She could see the exhaustion on his face and despite her resolve to feel nothing her heart went out to him. Billionaires could have problems, too. She didn't want to add to those worries so she decided to just state her situation in a matter-of-fact way and let Dare know he would not need to be involved in any way.

"My friend, Robyn, called today and she'd love to come to visit me. We haven't seen each other in a while. We'll be busy catching up on old times so we won't get in your way." Erin threw it all out there, watching him intently the whole time, trying to gauge his reaction.

Dare shrugged then stifled a yawn. "It doesn't matter to me just as long as you don't expect me to be here to do entertaining. Now isn't the time."

"Not at all," Erin said, relieved he had no objections. One less thing to worry about. "You won't even know we're here."

"I doubt that," he said with a crooked smile. Then his eyes settled on her and for the first time that night she felt that he was really seeing her. All week he'd been distant, almost like a visitor in his own home, leaving early and coming in hours after the sun had set. Now, though, he was here in the flesh and all of his attention was on her.

"How are you feeling, Erin?"

"I'm fine," she said, feeling her face redden. It was a reasonable question so why did it make her nervous?

He was silent for a moment, his eyes never leaving hers. Then he reached across the table and took her hand in his.

She jumped. His touch was so unexpected. Surreptitiously, she sucked in some air in an effort to slow her racing pulse. She was dying to pull her hands back but she didn't.

"Are you?" he asked, and the words were more seduction than question. Even as his fingers formed a band of steel around her wrist his thumb was doing a slow, sensual caress in the middle of her palm.

Erin dropped her gaze, trying to hide the effect he was having on her. She struggled to breathe normally but when his thumb left her palm to stroke the throbbing pulse point at her wrist her breath caught in her throat. And she grew moist. Her body was ready and willing even if she wasn't.

"I haven't been treating you very well, have I?" His voice soft and low, he was watching her with hooded eyes. "My brand new wife, home and all alone."

"I wasn't alone. I had Francine," she said, her voice strained, and she tried to pull her hand away. He did not let go.

"Francine," he said with a low chuckle. "Can Francine make your pulse race like it's doing now? Can she steal your breath away like this?"

Before Erin could decipher his cryptic message, Dare was on his feet pulling her into his arms. He dipped his head and captured her mouth with his and kissed her until she swayed and leaned into him. She had no choice. The man had caught her off guard, infiltrated her ranks before she'd had a chance to shore up her defenses. All her well-made plans, all her schemes to resist him were dashed with one fell kiss.

Dare lifted his head and stared into her eyes, his fingers moving quickly. He was untying her sash and loosening the buttons of her top.

Erin gripped his wrist, trying to still his hands. She had to regain her sanity. "Dare, no. We can't-" She gasped, unable to say more.

Dare had sat back down on the chair, leaving her standing, and now he had her nipple between his teeth.

Oh, Lord, how was she going to resist? He was sucking on her nipple now, and her hands that had tried to restrain him fell away, leaving him to do as he pleased. When his heated palms slid up her back, her body shuddered with the feel of his caress and she moaned.

Of their own volition her hands went up to cup Dare's head and pull him into her, the better to savor his sweet seduction.

Finally, Dare released her but only long enough to push her pajama top and robe off her shoulders and pull her onto his lap. If she'd had any doubts about the state of his arousal they were dismissed immediately. The hardness that pressed up through the cotton fabric of her pajama bottom was testament to the depth of his desire.

Now totally bare from the waist up, Erin felt a wave of embarrassment wash over her and she turned to bury her face in Dare's neck. She turned her body toward him, clinging to his shirt, trying to hide herself from his gaze.

Her body had changed and her heart faltered as she wondered how he would react. Her breasts had grown fuller, riper and so much more sensitive. The slightest touch sent thrills coursing through her body. But her waist had thickened and she could no longer close the button on her jeans. How would he see her now?

Her face still hidden, Erin could feel Dare's hands roaming over her body. She was not seeing, just feeling - the warmth of his body against hers, his big hands cupping her breasts, his fingers teasing her nipples - and the sensations were so intense that she moaned.

"You're so beautiful."

Dare's hoarse whisper was like a song to her heart and she sighed and relaxed in his arms.

"Come," he said then lifted her into his arms and stood. "It's time I had a real taste of my lovely wife."

At his words Erin's eyes widened and she laid a hand on his chest. "Dare, no. You promised."

He was heading out of the kitchen now, carrying her as if she were nothing but a small child. "Promised what?"

"This marriage. It's in name only," she said as she began to wriggle in his arms. She wanted him to put her down. How firm and businesslike could she be when he was holding her so close she could hear his heart beating in her ear? No, she needed to be on solid footing to have this conversation.

"In name only." He gave a harsh laugh. "You've got to be kidding." He kept on walking, totally ignoring her struggle to get down.

"Put me down." Erin spoke through clenched teeth and gave him a punch on the arm. He didn't even flinch. "I'm not going anywhere with you."

That brought another laugh from Dare. "You seem to be coming along quite nicely."

"Dare, if you don't put me down this instant I'm going to scream and you're not going to like it."

"Go ahead. Scream all you want. Francine is all the way in the far wing of the house and she sleeps like a log."

By this time they were in a part of the house to which Erin had never ventured. They were approaching Dare's suite. She had to do everything in her power to stay out of his room. Once inside, she would be lost. She had to make him stop.

"Dare DeSouza if you don't put me down I'm going to scream bloody murder." She was determined that she would not cross his threshold. He'd rejected her once. She would never, ever give him the opportunity to do it again. She drew for the one thing she knew was guaranteed to make him stop. "Are you so desperate you're resorting to rape?"

If she'd shot him in the chest with a bullet it could not have halted him faster. Dare came to a sudden stop and, his face black as midnight, he stared down at her. "What the hell did you just say?"

Erin dropped her eyes and bit her lower lip. She didn't need to repeat herself. He'd heard her loud and clear. And her plan had worked.

Dare slid his arm from beneath her legs and lowered her to the ground. Once he'd set her on her feet he stepped back and his look was dark with displeasure.

"I want you, Erin. Make no mistake about that. But I'll be damned if I'll be accused of rape." He folded his arms across his chest. "I may want you but I will never force myself on you." His gray eyes turned cold. "Next time, you'll have to be the one to make the first move. I won't lay a finger on you unless you come to me. Begging."

With that, he turned on his heels and walked away, leaving her standing there, her arms still wrapped around her chest.

She'd made her point and he'd gotten the message. Mission accomplished. So why did she feel like her life had just ended?

Slowly she turned and walked back to the kitchen. As she dressed an unexpected tear slid down her cheek.

With a sniff she wiped it away with the back of her hand, disgusted with herself for this display of weakness. If she was going to survive under Dare DeSouza's roof she'd better develop a backbone.

And if she was going to survive a week with Robyn she'd better return to all she'd learned about suppressing her emotions.

Between Dare and Robyn she was going to have a heck of a time controlling those emotions. Under no circumstances could she afford to crumble in front of either one of them. She would have to call on all her reserves to survive the week. God help her.

CHAPTER EIGHT

After a near sleepless night Dare headed out early the next morning. He'd scheduled a meeting with a private investigator and he was anxious to get an update on the findings.

When the man was ushered into his office at eight thirty that morning he was standing by the desk, ready for the news. He practically paced a trail into the carpet, waiting for him.

They shook hands then he offered Paul Ogilvie a seat. The big man's frame swallowed up the chair.

He began without preamble. "I'm afraid it's not good news, Mr. Desouza."

Dare's lips tightened but he nodded. He'd been hoping for the best, that he'd find some way to redeem his long-time friend and absolve him from any wrongdoing, but it was not to be.

"Bart Reynolds had a serious conflict of interest in this deal." The blond giant leaned over and dropped a large brown envelope in the center of Dare's desk. "It's all there. He was a primary shareholder in that property with full knowledge of its dilapidated state. You did him a favor in taking it off his hands."

The news almost floored Dare. So that was why Bart had pushed him so hard on this deal, giving him all kinds of assurances. The bastard.

Then he thought of something. "Wait a minute. You said the buildings were dilapidated but I didn't see any evidence of that."

"Bart took you on that tour of the property, right?"

Dare nodded.

"Just as I thought." Ogilvie's face was grim. "He deliberately took you to the sections that had been spruced up for your visit. Half of those structures are hollow shells, eaten out by wood termites. He wouldn't have taken you to those."

Dare puffed out his cheeks and blew out his breath. So that was it. He'd put all his trust in Bart and had been taken for a hell of a ride. If he couldn't trust a friend of over ten years who in the world could he trust? "So where is he now?"

"Last information we got he'd left the island for the south of France with a former model on his arm. He set himself up for a pretty sweet life."

"And this is?" Dare jerked his head toward the envelope.

"Photos, bank records, papers showing his connection to the property." The P.I. shrugged. "Nothing I haven't already told you. They're just for your records."

There was nothing more to be said. Nothing more to be done. He probably didn't even have the option of suing. He'd signed in good faith and now he was paying a high price for his trust.

"Thank you for your help."

As Dare held out his hand Paul Ogilvie stood and shook it. "Any time, Mr. DeSouza. If you need any more checks done you know where to find me."

Dare nodded and gave a grunt of acknowledgement. That was as much as he could manage.

Right now his mind was consumed with the issue at hand - how in the blazes to recoup two hundred and fifty million dollars.

***

Erin tapped her rolled-up magazine against her leg as she waited for Robyn to exit the customs and immigration department. The days had flown by much too fast and Sunday had arrived, bold and bright, the day her nemesis would appear. When the flight arrived crowds of people came through the doors, people waving to family members who had come to pick them up and professionals decked out in business wear. This went on for almost an hour and still there was no sign of Robyn. And there was no answer from her cell phone.

Finally, when Erin had paced the airport lobby for the umpteenth time, she heard a squeal.

"Darling. There you are."

She turned to see a bundle of red rushing through the double doors followed by a porter pushing a trolley with bags that looked like they had enough clothes for a year-long stay.

Within seconds Robyn was upon her, kissing her on both cheeks. "You're looking so good," the redhead said with a laugh. "And you've put on weight. Married life agrees with you."

Erin stepped back and adjusted her loose jacket so that it fell away from her body. Robyn didn't know she was pregnant but she would, soon enough. But now was not the time. She'd let the girl gloat, thinking she'd simply grown plump from lack of exercise. She pasted a smile on her lips and looked Robyn up and down, from the red beret on her head to her red suit and matching shoes. She looked almost European in her elegant pencil skirt. She must be going through one of her European phases. At times she considered things European to be en vogue and so she dressed the part and even adopted their accents and expressions.

"You look beautiful, as usual," she told Robyn and watched her face light up even more. She never tired of receiving compliments.

"Thank you," she said and looked around. "So where's that husband of yours?"

"Aah, he's very busy at the moment. Our chauffeur will take us home." As she spoke she dug into her purse for her cell phone. She'd have to call for the car to come around.

Robyn's mouth set in a pout she probably thought was cute. "Aaw, I was looking forward to meeting him."

"You will," Erin said. "Soon." That was what she told Robyn but, in truth, she wished to delay that meeting as long as possible. Robyn was a notorious man stealer and the fact that this was a married man was little consolation. Everyone was fair game on her playing field.

Within minutes the chauffeur was loading the bags, five in all, into the trunk and then they were off, the serpent and the little mouse eyeing each other. Erin almost laughed as the image flashed through her mind. Would there ever come a day when she didn't feel intimidated by Robyn?

That night, and much to Erin's relief, Dare did not make an appearance before bedtime. Robyn's disappointment was palpable. The girl's true colors began to show through her façade when she snapped at Francine during the evening meal.

"Why does she keep hovering around?" she complained as Francine came in to check on them for the third time. "It's so annoying."

"Francine's a lovely woman," Erin said in defense. "She's just a little overprotective, that's all. She's the motherly type."

"Well, she'd better not try to bother me. She's only the hired help, after all." This was followed by a toss of her head.

Erin didn't think Robyn had to worry about more mothering. Francine had been just about to enter the room when she was stopped by Robyn's outburst. The older woman's face fell and she disappeared back down the hallway. Erin could only hope she didn't think she shared Robyn's opinion.

When she finally bid Robyn goodnight and closed the door to the guest quarters she could only sigh in exhaustion and relief. One night down, five more to go.

Another day passed without incident, with Erin taking Robyn shopping at the boutiques scattered around the town's center, and having her walking from store to store until she was beat. By the time they got home Robyn crashed, totally exhausted.

By the third day, though, the visitor was determined that her trip to the island would not be in vain. At least that was how it seemed to Erin. Robyn got up with the rising of the sun and knocked on her door. Not waiting for an answer, she popped her head around the door.

"Wake up, sleepy head," she said, her smile falsely bright and cheerful. "Let's have an early breakfast."

Erin looked at her through eyes still blurry from sleep. "Francine isn't up yet," she said in an attempt to protest.

"Who needs Francine? We'll make our own breakfast."

Erin was not fooled. Robyn hadn't suddenly developed a love for the fresh early morning air. No, her goal was to meet Dare. This time there would be no way to keep them apart.

As per Robyn's plan, both women were sitting at the breakfast table when Dare walked in looking breathtakingly handsome in dark business suit and maroon-colored tie.

"Good morning, ladies." He walked over to Erin and leaned down to give her a peck on the cheek. He smelled of an ocean-breeze aftershave lotion. "How are you today?" He gave her a loving look.

Erin almost laughed. She'd had no idea he was such a good actor. "Just fine, honey," she said, her voice sugary-sweet. Two could play that game. She smiled and looked across at Robyn whose face sported a bright and very false smile. "Dare, I would like you to meet my friend, Robyn."

Dare gave a chivalrous bow and took Robyn's proffered hand. He bent his head and kissed the back of it and she gave a girlish giggle.

Erin almost rolled her eyes. Please.

Dare released her hand then gave her an apologetic look. "You've been here two days and I'm just getting the chance to meet you. My apologies. My work has kept me very busy these last few days."

"Oh, not at all," Robyn said with a wave of her hand. "I know how it is. You have to make the money, right?" She gave a tinkly laugh. "But I hope you'll be here for dinner this evening. After all, you can't work all the time." She cocked her head in her classic Robyn pose, the one where she added a slightly pouty mouth that men thought was cute.

Dare gave a slight nod. "I'll do my best to fulfill my duties as your host."

That got a smile of celebration from Robyn. "I look forward to getting know you." The way she said the words, so low and seductive, left no room for doubt as to her meaning.

Erin felt a slow heat rising from her belly but Dare seemed to take things in stride.

"I'm sorry I won't be able to join you for breakfast." He was reaching for an apple as he spoke. "I'll just munch this on the way.

Enjoy your day." With that he was gone, leaving the women alone in the room.

"What was that all about?" Erin hissed.

"What?" Robyn's face was all innocence.

"You know what. You were flirting with Dare. He's supposed to be my husband, remember?"

"Supposed to be?" Robyn lifted an eyebrow. "Sounds to me like you're not sure. Maybe you're in over your head?"

Erin frowned. "What's that supposed to mean?"

"It means, what's a girl like you doing with a man like him? You're not even in the same class."

So there it was. The gloves were off now. No need for pretenses anymore. The fight was out in the open.

"You don't know anything about money," Robyn continued, the veil gone from her face now contorted with spite. "You're out of your league here."

Erin felt her heart tighten. It was true. She was like an alien in this world of riches. But still, Robyn had no right. "He's my husband," she said finally, her voice strong and defiant. "No matter what you may think, he's mine and I'm part of his world."

"We'll see about that." Robyn sat back in her chair, her expression smug.

"Meaning?"

"Meaning we'll just see how long your husband keeps you here once he finds out about the real you."

Erin gasped. "You wouldn't."

"Try me," Robyn smirked.

"You would break up a marriage just to soothe your ego?"

"I just want Dare to know exactly who he married. That's only fair."

Erin took a deep breath. The nightmare had begun and it was far worse than she'd expected. She knew Robyn had not come to the island to be supportive. She'd even expected a little flirtation, but this? To threaten to reveal a secret she'd shared in confidence, a secret that could jeopardize her marriage?

She decided to use her wild card. Her face calm, she looked Robyn in the eyes. "You would break up a marriage even though I'm expecting Dare's child?"

That did the trick. Robyn stared at her, her face frozen in shock. "You're pregnant?"

In answer Erin got up and unbuttoned the loose jacket she'd been using to hide her condition. The bump in her belly was now obvious through the cotton fabric of her blouse.

"My God." Robyn looked at her belly and her face grew red. "How could I have missed that?"

The tension was suddenly too much for Erin. She walked over to the counter as a sudden wave of nausea washed over her. She sucked in a deep breath, willing her churning stomach to settle. She couldn't afford to show weakness. Not now.

She had her head down when she heard Robyn's voice again. It seemed to be coming from far away. "Now I see what happened. You devious little witch. You knew exactly what you were doing, didn't you?"

The venom in the woman's voice was like a knife thrust into Erin's belly. Why did Robyn hate her so much? With shaking hands she reached up and took a glass from the cupboard then filled it from the tap. She took a few sips then drew in her breath and turned around. Now she was ready.

"Robyn, I don't know what I was thinking when I allowed you to come here. Obviously it was a big mistake. I want you to leave."

Erin made her voice strong and bold even though she felt almost ready to pass out.

"You...want me to leave?" Robyn spluttered. "You're throwing me out?"

"Yes," Erin said, her voice surprisingly calm. "You came here knowing that you held the handle while I was holding the blade. You planned to use that against me, make me submit to your desires, even if it meant flirting with my husband. Even stealing him. It's not going to happen."

Robyn pushed her chair back, making a long scraping sound on the marble tiles. "Oh, so we're tough now, are we? Don't care about our reputation anymore? One word from me and this doll's house can come tumbling down around your ears."

The nausea was coming back. Beads of perspiration popped out on Erin's brow and again she had to turn away. She couldn't take this, not now, not in her condition. "Robyn," she whispered as she struggled to keep her breakfast down, "please leave."

As Robyn stormed out of the room Erin held on to the counter then made her way back to the table where she sank gratefully into the chair. She sat there for a while gulping in air then she gathered just enough strength to get up and grab a can of ginger ale from the fridge. It was the only thing guaranteed to dispel her nausea.

It took a whole ten minutes for Erin to return to normal. Still, she did not move. She sat there thinking. And thinking.

What was she going to do now? She'd just upset - no, angered - the one person in the world with the power to create a mess of her life. Well, the one person outside of Dare DeSouza. She had created a real enemy.

She clenched her fists in her lap. Whatever Robyn chose to do she would have to deal with it even if it meant that she ended up on the street. But there was no way she would continue to live under that witch's control.

Her mind made up, Erin got up and went to find the chauffeur. Robyn would need the ride back to the airport.

CHAPTER NINE

Dare sank into the seat of the town car and, eyes closed, rested his head against the back. It had been another rough day. They hadn't had any luck in locating Bart Reynolds in Europe. What was the use, anyway? The contract he'd signed was airtight. Two hundred and fifty million. Down the drain, just like that. It was a lot of money to lose.

Dare knew he would recover from this loss. He always did. If there was one thing he knew it was how to fail and keep on coming back. Wasn't that the common factor linking all successful entrepreneurs?

He sighed. Maybe it was a good thing he'd decided to make it an early night. He'd as much as promised Erin's friend that he would have dinner with them and he meant to keep that promise. But God, he was dead tired. He hadn't even bothered to drive himself home. As soon as he called, Carlos had come out to get him. He'd arrived before Dare even had the chance to stuff his papers into his briefcase. Thank God for reliable employees.

Once at home, a brisk shower was all it took to get him back to normal. Dressed in comfortable slacks and a light silk shirt he headed for the dining room where dinner would be served at seven. He was prepared to be pleasant and accommodating, the perfect host. Erin's friend deserved at least that, if even for one evening. He knew Erin would be pleased he'd made the effort.

Erin. As his mind settled on her he shook his head. He could not figure her out. She'd thrown him for a loop when she'd adamantly refused him, even pissing him off by intimating that he would have to force her. He'd never forced himself on a woman in his life and he wasn't planning to start now.

But he would put that incident behind him. Tonight he'd be cool. Tonight it was all about the ladies.

The dining room was softly lit by elegant lamps positioned in the corners. A gold candelabra sat in the center of the table. And there, all alone, sat Erin.

Clearly, she didn't realize that he'd entered the room. Her eyes downcast, she seemed lost in thought. But what made him pause was the slight droop of her shoulders, a posture that spoke of sadness or pain. Even her mouth had lost its feisty pout.

"Erin." He said her name quietly but she jumped and jerked around to stare at him with her liquid amber eyes. Even there, in her eyes, he could see a strain that had not been there before. For some reason a feeling of guilt gripped him. Was he the cause?

"Are you all right?" He walked over and pulled out the chair at the end of the table, the one closest to her. He sat down and was just about to reach out and take her hand when he stopped. An innocent gesture but one she might misconstrue. He wasn't taking any chances.

She gave him a tiny smile and her eyes glittered in the candlelight. Or was that the glitter of tears? Dare could not tell but no matter what he was going through tonight he would be gentle with her. He knew he didn't have exclusive claim to problems. She was probably facing personal challenges of her own. And he could guess that being pregnant was no easy thing.

"I'm fine, Dare," she said, and her voice cracked on his name.

What the deuce had upset her so that she seemed on the verge of tears? "What's wrong, Erin? And where is your friend? Did something happen between the two of you?"

Erin tightened her lips then took a deep breath. "She had to go back to Vancouver earlier than planned. She's all right, though. She's fine."

"It's not her I'm worried about," Dare said, frowning. "I want to know about you. Did she upset you?"

Erin smiled again and shook her head but it was a sad smile and Dare was not fooled.

"Do you want to talk about it?" he asked, watching her intently.

"No, that's okay. Let's just eat." She picked up her napkin and rested it on her lap then looked at him expectantly.

He did the same but he had suddenly lost his appetite. Erin had been upset or hurt by Robyn whatever- her-name-was but obviously she wasn't comfortable talking about it. He would give her some space…for now. But damn if he wasn't going to get some answers. There was a lot about Erin that remained a mystery to him but he was going to get to the bottom of this one sooner rather than later.

They began to dine, in silence at first, and then slowly Erin began to relax in his presence. She popped an olive into her mouth, chewed and then looked over at him. "How did you manage to leave the office early today? You've been so busy with your project I didn't think you'd make it back in time for dinner."

"I promised," he reminded her. "Your friend made me."

At the mention of the recent departee her face clouded over but then it cleared and she was smiling again. "Well, I'm glad you made it."

Dare said nothing but he had to admit he felt good about it, too. Since he'd brought Erin back to the island he'd spent precious little time with her. Hell, they'd hardly exchanged words except for that time he'd tried to carry her off to his bed. And that had ended in disaster.

"And how's it going?" she asked. "Your project, is it almost completed?"

Now it was Dare's turn to look glum. He'd vowed not to even think about the damn thing tonight but now that Erin had brought it up all his anger came flooding back.

"Trust me," he said, "you don't want to know."

"Oh, but I do," she said quickly and reached out to touch his arm.

He dropped his eyes and looked at her hand and it looked so small and defenseless against the muscles of his arm. He was still staring at her hand when she pulled it away and in her eyes was a look of chagrin.

He could see that she was stiffening again and withdrawing into herself. He'd better start talking before she shut him out altogether. "Do you want the short version or the long version?" He said it with a smile, hoping to get her to relax again.

He knew he'd found success when she smiled again and said, "I'm not going anywhere. Let's have the long version."

And so it was that he told her about his two hundred and fifty million dollar dilemma.

"Oh, my God. Dare, you're joking." Her eyes were wide with wonder. "Right?"

He chuckled. "I wish."

"My God," she whispered, her eyes never leaving his face. "I can't even begin to imagine that amount of money. And you lost all that?"

He shrugged. "Pretty much. I still have the property but most of the buildings are only fit to be bulldozed. I guess I'll have to start from scratch with this one."

"Oh, no," she said then she looked back at him with a worried expression. "Does that mean you're bankrupt? Will you lose your house?"

She looked so distressed that Dare burst out laughing. "No need to worry your little head. You won't be put out on the street. I'll still be able to buy you little trinkets."

That got him a glare from Erin. "I'm not worried about me, you idiot. I'm worried about you. I'm used to being poor. You're not."

"So sweet of you, cherie," he said in a teasing tone, hoping to get another rise from her. She was so cute when she was angry. "But I'll be fine. It's a lot of money but it won't make me go broke."

"Wow." The word was filled with awe. "I can't imagine being so rich that I could say words like that."

"Oh, but you are, my dear."

"I'm what?"

"Rich. You're my wife. We didn't sign a prenuptial agreement so you are part owner of the estate." Then he looked at her through narrowed eyes, trying to gauge her reaction. "That's what you wanted, wasn't it?"

For a moment Erin stared at him, a confused look on her face, then as his meaning sank in her face turned red and she shot up from her chair. "Dare DeSouza, you're the one who came looking for me. You're the one who forced me to marry you so don't you accuse me of pursuing you for your money. You've got some nerve-"

"Okay, calm down. I was only joking." He reached out to grasp her wrist and tug gently until she sank back into her chair.

"Your joke was in bad taste."

"Yes, I can see that," he said, trying to look sorry although inside he was grinning. That had certainly put the pink back into her cheeks. He much preferred the passion of her anger to seeing her sad and defeated.

"But seriously," he continued, "do you know the worst part?"

"What? Isn't losing all that money the worst part?"

"No, losing a friend." He hoped she could see that this part was no joke. "I lost someone I've known for years, someone I thought I could trust." He clenched his fists and just stopped short of pounding it on the table. "If you can't rely on someone so close to you, who else can you trust?" He lifted his head and looked at her. "If there's one thing I expect from my friends it's honesty, you know?"

For a second Erin looked nonplussed then she nodded quickly but he could see the blood rising up her neck and to her cheeks. She looked like she wanted to say something but no words came. Instead she carefully placed her napkin beside her empty plate and for the second time that night she stood up. "I'm feeling a bit tired. I think I'll go to bed now."

She didn't even wait for him to reply. She walked away, leaving Dare staring after her in confusion.

Now what had he said to upset her? He shook his head. If he lived a million years he would never understand women.

***

After her dinner with Dare, Erin went back to her old strategy - avoid him as much as possible. That seemed to have been working fine until Robyn came and spoiled everything.

She knew she was being foolish but she still hadn't gotten over the shock of Dare's last statement at the dinner table. It was like he'd been talking about her. The guilt would not let her sit still and she'd had to leave as fast as she could before she broke down and told all.

It was five days since Robyn left the island and she hadn't heard a whisper since then. With each day that passed she breathed a sigh but she could guess that the girl would drop her bombshell at a strategic moment, at that point when it would hurt most. It was only a matter of time.

After a week passed and then two without any word from Robyn, the tension in Erin's belly began to dissipate. The threat still hung over her head but how long could she remain on edge? She willed herself to be calm. She had her baby to think about and she would not let anything - neither high blood pressure nor negative emotions - consume her and jeopardize the health of her unborn child.

She signed up for classes at the local Mommy Yoga Center and fell into a comfortable routine of yoga and birthing classes in the mornings and daily swims in the pool in the cool of the evenings. Eventually she stopped thinking about Robyn and the threat she posed.

With the passing of time Erin grew rounder and rounder until she looked like she had swallowed a basketball. When Dare teased her, calling her his panda bear, Francine came to her defense and laughingly found names for him, too. It didn't help that those names were in Spanish so Erin had no idea what she was talking about. She didn't care, though. It felt good to have another woman on her side. She and Dare fell into a comfortable rhythm that made Erin sometimes forget that her marriage was not quite the norm. From observing them no one would guess that their marriage was in name only.

Their idyllic life on the island hit a snag when it was announced that a hurricane was on the way. At the news Erin became filled with a sense of dread. She tackled Francine in the kitchen.

"What's a hurricane like? Will it destroy the island? Will we be in great danger?" The words shot out in rapid succession, clear evidence of her fright. She was not afraid to admit it. She'd never experienced a hurricane before and she was scared.

She'd heard horror stories of tidal waves taller than ten storey buildings and people getting sucked out to sea. She'd heard of heavy winds flattening houses, people getting electrocuted by downed power lines and people getting sick from contaminated water supplies. Nothing she'd heard about hurricanes was good.

"Ah, nina," Francine sighed, "hurricanes are dangerous but we will survive. And you, in this well built house, you will be safe. I'm happy that you have a strong man to protect you."

"But what about you, Francine? You will stay here with us, right? I want you to be safe." Erin grabbed the older woman's hand. Although Francine spent a lot of time in Dare's house she also had her own home on the island. Erin was worried that she would go back there. She could not explain it but she felt an affinity with Francine that was far more than an employer-employee relationship.

"No, nina. Senor Dare, he arranged for me to go to Atlanta to be with my son. I will leave long before the storm hits."

Erin breathed a sigh of relief. One less person to worry about.

Next day Erin accompanied Francine into the airport where they hugged and shared well wishes. The housekeeper waved goodbye as she stood at the entrance to the international departure lounge and her eyes glistened with tears. Erin, too, felt choked up but she bit her lip and held on. She would not give in to tears. She was not the emotional type and couldn't figure out why tears seemed to come so easily these days. It must be the baby hormones.

Erin spent the rest of the day shopping. Like everyone else she was making sure to have adequate supplies in case the hurricane devastated the island. It was not unheard of that, following a natural disaster such as this, electrical power would be out for weeks. With that in mind she stocked up on flashlights, lanterns and batteries, canned and packaged foods and dozens of cases of drinking water. When the chauffeur bundled her into the car to take her home there was hardly enough room left for her to sit. She didn't mind, though. She'd much rather be over prepared than in need.

That evening when Dare got home he told her he'd arranged for workmen to come in and board up the huge bay windows and French doors. The hurricane winds would easily shatter the panes, sending glass flying. They had to prevent that at all costs. He spoke calmly, almost casually, as if boarding up a house was the most natural thing to do. Meanwhile, Erin was quaking in her shoes.

Dare must have seen her fear because he stepped forward, looking like he was about to take her in his arms. But then he let his hands fall to his sides. Instead, he gave her a gentle smile. "It will be all right. This isn't the first hurricane to hit Santa Marta. We'll pull through just fine."

"But they say this will be the worst one in a decade. And what if we get a tidal wave? We're so close to the ocean." She spoke quietly, her voice steady, but she felt far from it. Her eyes searched his, desperately seeking the reassurance she needed right then. At that moment she would have welcomed his embrace so she could feel the strength and power of his body against hers and revel in the comfort of his arms.

But it was not to be. She'd set her boundary, one he'd vowed never to cross until she made the first move. And she wanted to. Even now as he stood looking down at her she wanted to.

But she could not.

Dare shoved his hands into his pockets and on his face was a look of determination. "We'll beat this, Erin. We just have to prepare the best way we can. I've already taken the necessary precautions at the resort. They're the ones that are close to the ocean, not us. This house is on a hill, remember?"

"You're right," Erin said, frowning. She hadn't thought about the resort at all. "What about the guests? How will they manage?"

"Half of them have already left and a few more will go tomorrow. For the ones who decided to stay we've moved them to the villas farthest from the beach. They'll be on a grade so they should be fine." He gave a sigh. "Thank God for loyal employees. We've got a skeleton staff staying on to serve them. They'll all be paid triple time for staying."

"Because they'll be away from their families?"

"Yes. I want them to know I appreciate the sacrifice they're making." He smiled. "They don't know it yet but I already spoke to the director of finance to factor in an extra bonus for them at the end of the year."

"That's generous of you," she said and her heart warmed to him. He'd been a jerk, no doubt about that, but after seeing this other side of him how could she stay mad?

And how could she stay unaffected by this enticingly sexy man? She'd vowed to keep saying no but with her pregnant hormones raging she seemed to constantly be in a heightened state of arousal. She wanted him so badly she could almost taste it.

But she had to stay strong. For the sake of her heart she could not put herself at risk a second time.

The next day dawned clear and bright. You would never know a hurricane was on the way. It was perfect weather for the workmen to complete their task and within just a few hours they were done.

That evening she and Dare went through their list of supplies, making sure they had everything they needed. At the last minute Dare remembered one critical piece - they hadn't checked the first aid kit. When they found it they realized that all the painkillers had expired and had to be thrown out. Dare made a quick dash to the local drug store, arriving just ten minutes before it closed. After that, with the kit filled with bandages, iodine for cuts and bruises, painkillers, gauze and a splint they were ready.

On the third day Erin and Dare woke to a sky that hung low and gray like an ominous shroud. Everywhere was still. There was no chirping or whistling in the trees this morning. Not a single bird had remained behind. Even the tree frogs seemed to have disappeared. The animals knew what was coming and they, too, had gone to seek shelter from the coming onslaught.

Even the air had stilled. Gone was the usual tropical breeze, the trade winds that would shake the leaves in the trees. It was as if they were in a vacuum-sealed flask.

Then the evening came and with it the first taste of what was to come. The air that had previously been so still now began to stir and within an hour of the first breeze a strong wind began to blow. With each passing hour it grew stronger until by nightfall the force of the wind had the palm trees bending low, practically kissing ground. What had started out as a whistling in the trees had now turned to a deafening howl that was almost human, making the hair on Erin's nape stand on end.

"Come," Dare said and she was grateful when this time he took her hand in his. His strength surged through her and she stepped closer to him.

Dare led her down the hallway and toward his suite and this time she was eager to go. There was a mighty beast outside pummeling the trees and battering the house and she was too frightened to stay alone.

They'd entered the sitting room and Dare was walking over to the table to rest the lantern down when a loud crack rent the air and the lights went out. Erin screamed and reached blindly for Dare.

"It's okay, Erin, it's okay." His voice came to her from across the room and then he was beside her, gathering her trembling body close to his.

"Wh…what was that?"

"Probably a tree uprooted by the wind. It sounded like it crashed into the house." Dare stroked her back as he spoke, soothing her jangling nerves. "I'm guessing it fell on a power line and that's why the lights went out. I'll go check-"

"Oh, no, you won't." Erin clung to him. "You're not leaving me in the dark all by myself."

"You'll be all right. I'll leave you with the lantern and take the flashlight."

"I'm coming with you. I'm not staying here."

"Erin," Dare said with an exasperated sigh, "you're safer here. I don't want you exposed to danger." As he spoke he reached behind his back to pry her fingers open. "I have to go check what's happening at the other end of the house."

He loosened her arms from around his waist and stepped away. Erin almost cried out but she bit down on her bottom lip and swallowed, containing the fright that threatened to creep up from the pit of her stomach. She pulled her robe tighter and went to stand beside Dare who was testing a huge flashlight.

He looked over at her when she came near. "Why don't you lie down for a bit? You have to take it easy, remember? You're in your sixth month now."

"That doesn't mean I'm an invalid," she retorted. "I don't need to lie down."

He reached out and rested a hand on her shoulder. "I want you to. You can have the loveseat or just go into my bedroom. You'll be a lot more comfortable there."

"In the dark? All by myself? I don't think so."

"We've discussed this already, Erin. You'll have the lantern-"

"No, I'm coming with you."

"Jeez." He blew out an exasperated breath. "Talk about stubborn. Okay, come on, but stay behind me at all times. When I open the door any kind of debris can fly in. I don't want you getting hurt."

"And what about you?"

"I can take care of myself."

Erin snorted. He'd spoken like a typical man. And that was why she was making sure to follow him. She'd be there to make sure he didn't do anything rash. He was a man and men did stupid things sometimes, thinking they were strong and brave and therefore near invincible. Well, not this time. She'd be there to save Dare from himself.

And it had absolutely nothing to do with being scared about being left alone with just a lantern as company.

With Dare in the lead Erin padded back down the hallway in her bedroom slippers even as the wind howled outside. The sound had gotten louder now, sounding like a huge freight train rushing by, and Erin's heart pounded harder with each passing minute. When would the assault end? Would the house still be standing when it was over? Would they still be alive?

That didn't even bear thinking about. She shook her head and kept on walking, making sure Dare was just within the reach of her arm.

When they got to the foyer he pulled out a second flashlight, clicked it on and handed it to her.

"I'm going over to the west wing to see what happened. You stay here." With those words he began to turn toward the hallway.

Erin grabbed his arm. "You said I could come with you."

"I know," he said, his face grim. "I changed my mind. There could be broken glass everywhere. The downed power line could have even started a fire. I don't want you anywhere near that." He shook his head. "I should have left you in the suite where you were safe."

"No, you shouldn't," she retorted. "You're not leaving me here so let's go." Before he could object she set off down the hallway, her flashlight on high beam, marching on as if the darkness ahead didn't bother her one bit. She breathed a sigh of relief when, with a grunt of what was probably exasperation, Dare followed her. As they walked Erin could feel a current of wind that flowed stronger and stronger as they went farther into that section of the house.

What she saw when they got to the west wing made her realize the reason for Dare's concern. The huge mango tree that used to stand by the window of Francine's bedroom had toppled over in the wind, smashing through the roof and leaving a gaping hole. The wind rushed through like air blown down a funnel, creating a miniature wind storm inside the room. As the beams from both flashlights lit up the area Erin could see papers, leaves and debris strewn all around and rain streaming in through the damaged roof.

"Jeez, this is bad," Dare murmured and stepped inside to get a better look.

A sudden gust of wind tore a plank from the jagged roof, sending it flying across the room.

"Watch out," Erin yelled.

Dare swiveled round, the light of his flashlight cutting through the air. He never even saw it coming. The plank slammed into Dare's side and smacked him on the head with a crack that echoed around the room. The flashlight was the first to fall. Then, like a hill of flour in a torrent of rain, Dare crumbled and collapsed onto the sodden floor.

"Dare!" Erin screamed but there was no answer. All she could hear was the deafening, diabolical roar of the hurricane winds.

CHAPTER TEN

"Oh, no," Erin cried out and ran to kneel at Dare's side. Her robe was immediately soaked with the water running freely on the floor. She shone the flashlight onto Dare and saw that he had fallen face down on the floor, water only inches from his nose. And he was not moving.

"Oh, God," Erin whispered. "God help me."

Quickly, she propped the flashlight on a pile of cushions nearby then reached for Dare, lifting his face clear of the water. Without hesitation she sat in the water and slid her legs under his head to lay it on her lap. Then, gently but urgently, she patted his face. "Dare, wake up. Please, honey. I need you to get up."

Her desperate pleas fell on deaf ears. Dare had been knocked unconscious.

Erin looked around, her mind racing. They could not stay there with water swirling around them and the shrieking wind threatening to pelt them with more debris. But what could she do? She couldn't possibly lift Dare but she couldn't leave him there either.

Then her eyes flew to the cover on the bed. If she could just roll him onto it then she could drag him out of the room and out of danger. Erin reached for a pillow that had fallen to the floor. Gently, she slid Dare's head from her lap and laid it on the soft support.

Slowly, she pulled her hand away and she almost cried out again. Her hand was smeared with blood. She had to move quickly. Dare was hurt even worse than she'd realized.

Braving the howling winds she half-dashed, half-waded to the bed in the middle of the room. The cover was soaking wet and heavy but she had no choice. She stripped the bed of its cover and dragged it over to where Dare lay. She spread it out on the ground then slowly, gingerly she lifted his head then she heaved and was just barely able to shift his head and torso onto the fabric. His bottom half was easier. When he was stretched out on the cover she propped the flashlight on his chest, angling it so it lit her path. Then she grabbed two handfuls of the cover and pulled. He did not budge. Kicking off her now sodden bedroom slippers she planted her feet on the ground and heaved. And that's when he began to move. Inch by inch she dragged Dare through the door and out into the hallway. Inch by inch she pulled him to safety.

By the time she got him out of the room and at a safe distance away she was panting from the effort. Unable to go further she slid down in a heap beside her prostrate husband.

Drawing up her legs she wrapped her arms around them and dropped her forehead onto her knees. What was she going to do now? Dare needed help but even if she got phone service what ambulance would come running in the middle of a hurricane? But what if he slept himself into a coma? Heavens, what was she to do? She couldn't just sit there all night.

Worn out with worry, a soft sob escaped Erin's lips and then another until she was sobbing in earnest. What made it worse, the harder she tried to stop the faster the tears came. Where had the practical levelheaded Erin gone? Pregnancy had turned her into a mountain of mush and she didn't like it, not one bit. But still she could not stop crying.

"Erin, are you all right?"

The sobs froze in Erin's throat. Her head snapped up and she peered down at Dare who was still stretched out on the cloth but this time his eyes were open. Those wonderful gray eyes were staring back at her.

"Dare," she said, her voice breaking, "you're back." She scrambled to her knees and reached over to gather him in her arms. When he flinched she drew back. "I'm sorry. I'll be gentle. I promise."

"It's okay," Dare said in a hoarse whisper. "I'm fine." His eyes roamed the hallway. "How did I get here?"

"I brought you out here," she said gently. "You were about to step into Francine's

room when a flying board slapped you. It knocked you out cold."

"And you…brought me out here?" He looked around then slowly raised himself on his elbows. "But how?"

Erin shrugged. "I dragged you out. On the blanket."

"You did what?" Dare's eyebrows shot up. He struggled to sit up then swayed and put a hand to the back of his head. "I got clobbered real good," he said with a groan.

"Yes you did, so move slowly. Very slowly." She put out a hand and gently held his chin then turned his head ever so slightly.

She shone the flashlight on his head. There was a gash at the back of it but thankfully it was not as bad as she'd expected and the blood had already begun to dry, matting the hair to his scalp. That was good. It would stem the flow.

Erin got up and held out both hands to Dare. "You're soaking wet. We have to get you dry before you fall sick."

"I can get up," he said, ignoring her outstretched hands. He put out a hand and, using the wall as support, slowly and carefully got up from the floor and stood looking down at her.

She could see he was far from steady. Without hesitation she went to stand beside him and pulled his arm across her shoulders. Then step by step they made their way to the safety of Dare's suite. There, Erin stripped him of every article of clothing then helped him into the bathroom where he washed away the grime from his recent repose in the pool of water on the floor.

Erin felt no embarrassment at Dare's nakedness. All such cares were swallowed up in her concern for him. With the dispassion of a nurse she toweled him dry then placed a robe around his shoulders and led him to the bed where she tucked him in.

Dare leaned back into the pillows with a sigh then looked over at her standing by the bed. "Thank you," he said. "You make an excellent nurse." Then he waved his hand toward a huge walk-in closet. "There's another robe hanging on the hook by the door. Why don't you change? You're all wet."

Erin didn't need to be told twice. She'd begun to shiver and she knew it was because of the damp clothes clinging to her body. She got the robe then went back to Dare's bathroom where she shed her garments and took a quick shower. Within a few minutes she was back at Dare's side.

The color had returned to his face and he was looking like his old self again, dark and deliciously sexy as the lantern cast its golden light on his bare chest. He'd pushed the robe away and now lay in the bed, naked from the waist up. And he was watching her. Those gray eyes like molten steel now bored into her, making her blush.

Slowly, suggestively he licked his lips and her nipples tightened in response. She breathed in, her nostrils flaring, and she clenched her hands by her side. What in heaven's name was he doing to her? Even in his wounded state he still had the power to seduce her.

Without a word and without a touch he was turning her insides to jelly.

And as the wind wailed its dirge outside Erin knew that at that moment what she wanted most was to be in Dare's arms.

Dare lifted his arms and folded them behind his head, looking very much like an overlord surveying his property. "What do you want, Erin?" he asked, his voice a bold and confident whisper.

He knew. Heaven help her, he knew how much she wanted him.

"Erin?" As he said her name he cocked an eyebrow, looking very much the rake.

She swallowed. Then she decided to take the plunge. She wanted him. So why should she deny herself?

"I want…you," she said, her voice thick with desire.

"Are you sure?" The look he gave her spoke volumes. She'd rebuffed him before and his look said he wasn't taking any chances.

"I'm sure," she said, her voice a wee bit stronger. Her body was clamoring for him and there was no denying it the release it craved. Not now, when her blood surged with the heat of passion. Certainly not now as the wind swirled outside, making her shiver for want of those muscled arms around her.

"Are you begging?" His eyes, glittering like diamonds in the light, danced with amusement.

She lowered her eyes and bit her bottom lip to keep it from trembling with laughter. Then she lifted her chin and looked him straight in the eyes. "I'm begging," she admitted and she said it without apology.

Dare's lips curled into a smile. He threw back the covers and held out his hands. "Come."

This time when Erin saw Dare's nakedness she felt the heat rush to her face. The Dare she had bathed was very different from the one who now lay bold and bare in front of her, that special part of his anatomy standing straight and proud.

After the trauma that the night had brought she needed him. And so, stifling the caution that would normally keep her in check, she climbed into Dare's bed and into his arms.

This time when they made love it was gentle and sweet. As she lay on her side in front of him he pressed himself against her back and wrapped his arms around her. When he kissed the back of her neck, sending shivers up her spine, she sighed and pushed back against him. When he cupped her breasts, now full and heavy in his hands, she arched her back and moaned until he pinched and rolled the taut nipples with his fingers, making her sweet spot moisten in response.

When he slid inside her, so thick and firm, her body was ready to receive him. Then his hand slid over her belly and down to her center of sensation and he began to stroke so softly like the touch of a feather then faster and faster, until all the colors of the rainbow exploded between her legs and shot like fireworks to every part of her body, making her cry out in release.

And as she reached her peak he pushed deep inside her, one long clean stroke, and then he was emptying his seed deep inside her.

For a long time they lay there, joined as one as they fought to regain control. Then as their harsh breathing died down to the gentle rhythm of satiation Dare gathered her even closer and slid his hand up to stroke the smooth skin of her hip.

And though the wind wailed and the windows rattled, Erin felt if there was one moment in life that defined her heaven, this was it.

But then she remembered. The wind, Francine's room, the plank flying through the air. She gasped and held Dare's wrist, stilling his caress. "Dare, your head. What if I made you worse?"

Dare chuckled into the back of her neck. "By letting me make love to you? You actually did the opposite. I'm cured."

She reached behind and slapped at his bum. "Be serious. You could have a concussion. I don't think making love was a good idea."

"It was an excellent idea," he whispered then kissed her nape, effectively wiping all thought from her mind and leaving her only with the feel of his body and his touch.

Then he turned her to him and dipped his head to confound her even further with a kiss that left her panting.

She lifted her hands and planted them on his chest. "Dare, no. I mean it. No more for tonight. Not in your condition."

He chuckled and leaned back and propped his elbow on the pillow then rested his cheek in his hand. He gave her a boyish grin. "Or in yours." He reached out and rested a big warm hand on her belly. "I hope I didn't disturb little Mr. DeSouza."

"Or Miss," she said, smiling back.

"Or Miss." He stroked her smooth skin then lowered his head to press his ear against her gentle rise. "I wish I could hear it," he said, his voice soft with something akin to wonder.

"Why don't you say something?" she prompted. "The baby can hear, you know."

To her surprise, instead of speaking Dare began to sing, soft and low, his voice a melodic rumble as his lips tickled the skin of her belly. He was singing a lullaby to the baby inside her, a song welcoming the little one into the world.

As the words of the song died away Erin blinked to clear the tears that had gathered in her eyes. It had been so unexpected and so touching. "That was beautiful," she said and raised her hand to stroke Dare's dark curls as he again pressed his ear against her skin. It felt so natural. "I didn't know you could sing."

He lifted his head and chuckled. "I was part of a boy band in college. Bass guitarist and background vocalist."

"Wow," she said with a teasing laugh, "you never cease to amaze me. If you hadn't made it in real estate you would definitely have made it big in the music business."

"Yeah, right." He slid his body up where he could nuzzle her neck. She knew what he wanted and this time she didn't have the heart to stop him. Crack on the head or no, Dare - or more accurately the part of his anatomy now prodding her hip - was ready for another round.

She sighed and stretched languorously then tilted her head up and gave him a peck on the cheek. "Just one more time," she whispered, "but only if you sing me a love song."

"Are you begging?" he said into her ear.

"No, that was an order." She reached up and pulled his head down for a long, searing kiss that would leave him in no doubt as to who was in charge.

CHAPTER ELEVEN

Dare woke to a ray of light streaming in through a crack in the brocade drapes at the window. For the first time in weeks he'd slept through the night. He lifted his head off the pillow to look at his wife as she curled into him. She was still fast asleep and he used the opportunity to explore her body with his hand, sliding it over the fullness of her breasts then letting it come to rest in the curve of her waist. She was beautiful in her pregnancy, her skin a delicate rosy hue, her body blooming with his child. What could be lovelier?

If nothing else, the hurricane had accomplished one good thing. Last night they had connected. For the first time since Erin's arrival on the island there had been a harmony between them that he hoped would last. He would do everything in his power to maintain this newfound peace. He'd been a cad but going forward he'd show Erin he could be a loving husband.

Slowly, so as not to wake her, he slid out of the bed and padded over to the walk-in closet where he grabbed underwear, jeans, a T-shirt and a pair of heavy boots. All kinds of debris would be strewn around after the storm, including broken glass and loose boards with nails sticking out. The last thing he needed was a puncture wound that would send him rushing to the hospital for a tetanus shot.

A quick survey of the grounds revealed that the damage was not as bad as he had expected. Apart from the tree that had fallen onto the west wing of the house everything else was intact. Still, it was going to take a lot of work to clear the mess from the property. He'd have to get a work team on board within the next day or two.

His priority, though, was the resort and the guests who were in his care. A quick call to the resort manager put his mind at ease - all guests present and accounted for and only minor damage to the villas closest to the beach.

He went back to check on Erin and she was up. She'd put on his robe again and it swallowed her up, making her look like a child playing dress up in her parents' clothes.

As soon as she saw him her face lit up and then it clouded over with a look of concern. "How do you feel today?" she asked. She hopped out of the bed and came over to rest a hand on his arm. "Any headaches? Dizziness?"

"I'm fine, nurse," he teased then reached out and pulled her against him. "And how did you rest?"

"Never slept better," she said with a relaxed smile and then her face went pink and he knew she was remembering their lovemaking from the night before.

And she'd soon have a lot more to grow pink about. Tonight he planned to give her even more of the same treatment. But now there was work to do. "You whip up some breakfast while I make some calls and get a work crew organized. It's going to be a busy day."

"Not for you, it's not," she said, her eyes flashing. "Your first order of business is to swing by the hospital and have them check out that bump on your head."

"But-"

"Not another word, mister. Go freshen up while I make breakfast. Then it's off to the doctor for you."

Dare could only stare at her in amused surprise. Now where had this bossy spirit come from? There was a lot more to Erin than met the eye.

As much as he wanted to get started on the repairs he realized the wisdom of her words. With a nod and a quick grin he yielded to his new boss and headed off to the bathroom.

Later that morning with the permission of his doctor Dare made his rounds of the resort and ensured that competent staff was on hand to cater to the guests. Then he stopped by his office to make some important phone calls after the storm. He had to connect with his relatives back in Michigan to assure them he was safe and with his insurance company to arrange for an assessment of the damage. It was a good thing he'd included flood insurance and wind damage for all his properties.

When he got back home late that afternoon Erin was nowhere to be found. He called her cell phone.

"There was an announcement on the radio that the shelter got a lot more people than they bargained for. They've run out of blankets so I got Carlos to take me down here to drop some off." There was the sound of static and then her voice came back on the line but weaker than before. "It's really bad, Dare. Lots of damage-" The call dropped, leaving him clutching the phone to his ear.

He tried calling back but only got a busy signal. Obviously, the hurricane had not only affected the electricity supply. It had messed up the phone systems, too.

He just hoped she would hurry back. She was in no condition to be traipsing all over town trying to save the world.

Within an hour Erin was back home looking flushed and eager. "They were so happy for the blankets," she said, beaming. "We should take them some food, too. With all the people who turned up at the shelter I'm sure they'd appreciate it."

"Sure," Dare said, taking her by the shoulder and leading her over to the reclining chair. "But not today. You need to put your feet up and relax. Remember what the doctor said about the swelling in your ankles."

"He said I need exercise, not pampering." But despite her protest she relaxed into the chair and put her feet up, much to his relief.

He could see how much it meant to her to have been able to render assistance. She was obviously a kindhearted soul and he loved her for it.

Dare paused and looked up from where he was kneeling at her feet. Love. Now where had that thought come from? Unbidden, it had popped into his mind, startling him with how easily it had slipped in. Did he love Erin?

If his actions were anything to go by then maybe it was so. Right then he was busy massaging her ankles, helping to stimulate the circulation and prevent swelling. It made him feel...husbandly, if that was a word. But he had to admit, something had changed. He still wanted Erin, that was for sure, but that alone was no longer enough. His feelings for her had blossomed into something far more than just the physical. Now his desire was for an emotional connection.

That evening Dare made his specialty, stir-fried chicken with white rice, and he and Erin sat down to a quiet meal alone. They finished off with a cup of herbal tea for Erin and black coffee for Dare. Then, for the first time since they'd met, he told her about his musical family. He talked about his dad, a country and western singer who had moved to Michigan with his young wife, where they'd performed in nightclubs across the city.

As teenagers Dare and his two brothers often joined their parents on stage. Later, one of his brothers went on to a musical career while the other became a psychiatrist. Dare chose the field of engineering.

"But the entrepreneurial spirit won out, I see." Erin lifted her teacup to him.

Dare nodded. "Never even got the chance to use my engineering degree, but who's complaining?"

They were both having a laugh at that when Dare's cell phone began to buzz. He peered at the screen. "My broker. Calling me now? Weird." He took the call and was on the phone less than two minutes when he hung up. He was all smiles.

"Did you just win the lottery?" Erin asked cheekily. A man like Dare probably never wasted his time or his money on such slim odds.

"Better. That was my insurance broker. He said they'll be going out tomorrow to assess the property damage at that new resort I bought. It's likely they'll cover up to eighty percent of the damage."

"But why not one hundred percent?"

"That would be the ideal but there's that pesky little thing called the deductible they have to take out first." He shrugged. "But the good thing is, Dennis went to look at the place and the bulk of the wind damage was to those villas I was planning to bulldoze anyway. They were too hollow to stand up to the hurricane."

"A blessing in disguise," she murmured.

"You got that right." Then he gave her a naughty look. "To celebrate I'll grant you one wish, anything you want."

"A massage," she said with delight. "I want you to massage me from head to toe. Carrying this weight around is hard on the back and the legs."

He put on a disappointed look. "Nothing else? Just a massage?"

"Yes, Dare," she said, rolling her eyes, "just a massage. We've had enough fun for a while, don't you think?"

He didn't press after that. Erin had been more than generous in that department, considering her condition. He would give her a well-deserved break. He gathered the cups and teapot onto the tray. "Be right back," he said and headed for the kitchen.

Dare had just deposited the tray onto the marble countertop when he heard a yell. It was Erin and she was shouting his name. He jogged back to the sitting room to see what the fuss was about.

What Dare saw made his blood run cold. Erin had collapsed onto the floor. She was clutching her stomach and moaning.

He rushed over to kneel by her side. "What's wrong?'

"Cramps," she gasped, her brow beaded with perspiration. She gritted her teeth and clutched his hand with a strength that rivaled a weight lifter's. "I think…I'm going into labor."

"Labor?" he all but shouted. "You're nowhere near due yet."

"Tell that to the baby," she half-laughed half-groaned, then she was clutching his shoulders with both hands, shivering with the pain that shot through her body.

"We're going to the hospital," he said and lifted her into his arms.

"I'm not dressed," she gasped. "My bag. It's not packed."

"Forget all that, Erin. We have to go now." His heart pounded so hard it hurt. What the hell was going on? Erin hadn't even hit her seventh month yet. How could she be having contractions? He placed her in the back seat where she could have more room to stretch out then he jumped into the Jaguar and speed off to the same hospital he'd visited just hours before.

As soon as they rushed into the emergency room Erin was wheeled off to a private room where the doctor on duty did an assessment. That was when they realized that Erin had been spotting.

"What does it mean?" she asked, her eyes wide as she clung to Dare's hand. "Am I going to lose my baby?"

The doctor patted her hand. "We'll run some tests then we'll see what's going on." He waved his hand to a waiting orderly. "Ultrasound department," he said and the man came forward at once to take Erin away in her wheelchair.

Dare was right behind him. "I'm coming, too," he said. There was no way he was going to allow them to take Erin out of his sight. But there was something weighing on his mind, something he just could not shake. As he followed the men he cleared his throat. "Doctor," he said, "if she…exerted herself, could that cause her to lose the baby?"

"These things can happen," the doctor said with a nod. "But what kind of exertion are you speaking of?"

"Exertion of the…sexual kind." Dare could not believe he was feeling embarrassed to speak to the doctor about something as normal as sex between two married people.

"That shouldn't be a problem as long as you're careful," the doctor replied. "Now if she had other kinds of exertion that's a whole different matter. Did she do anything out of the ordinary? Lift anything heavy, perhaps?"

Dare's heart gave a jolt. How could he have forgotten? "Yes," he said as a feeling of guilt washed over him. "Me."

"You?" The doctor looked at him as if he'd gone mad.

"I was knocked unconscious during the hurricane," Dare told him. "She rolled me onto a bedcover and dragged me out of a bedroom and down a hallway."

"Down a…" The look the doctor gave him was one of incredulity. "She didn't."

"I'm sorry to say, she did." Dare's voice was quiet, his thoughts far away. This was his fault. If anything happened to Erin or the baby he would never forgive himself. "And she didn't complain of any pains at the time?"

"No, nothing." Dare shook his head. "We even made love after that."

The doctor let his breath out with a huff and Dare didn't know if it was out of disbelief or disgust. He wouldn't blame him for judging. He was disgusted with himself. What kind of husband was he to put his pregnant wife through all of that?

"She's a strong woman, Mr. DeSouza," the doctor said. "I can see it in her. And we will do all that we can for her and the baby."

All that we can. He hadn't said they'd be fine. He'd given no assurances. That was not what Dare wanted to hear.

When they got to the ultrasound room they wheeled Erin in and Dare went to follow but the doctor put up his hand. "I'm sorry but it's very cramped in here. The technologist needs the limited space to work and I need to be there to see what's going on. Could you wait over there, please?" He pointed to a row of chairs along a nearby wall.

Dare felt like throttling him. It must have shown on his face because the doctor backed away then quickly pushed the door shut. Dare slapped the wall with his open palm. He would have preferred to put his fists through the wall, he was so frustrated. He needed to be there for Erin. He needed to hold her hand, give her his strength, be her support. Suppose she called out for him? And he needed to see what was going on with his baby.

He walked over to the row of chairs but could not sit. Instead, he paced up and down and then stopped in front of the closed door then paced up and down some more. He looked at his watch. He couldn't believe only three minutes had passed. He checked the time on his cell phone, not believing, but yes it was correct. Damn. How long would he have to wait? This waiting was driving him crazy.

He stepped away from the door and paced some more. He was on his sixth trip to the door when it popped open. Erin was back but this time on a stretcher and her eyes were full of tears. Dare went to her and as soon as she saw him the tears began to flow freely.

"The baby is in distress. He can't survive inside me. They have to take him." She began to sob and as she stretched out her hand to him Dare felt powerless. All he could do was take her in his arms and hold her while she cried. A tap on his shoulder jerked him out of his pain. He turned to see the doctor at his side.

"Please. We need to get to the operating room right away. Emergency C-section."

Then before he could do more than plant a kiss on Erin's forehead they were wheeling her away, leaving him standing alone in the middle of the corridor.

Then followed the worst two hours of Dare's life. Other patients were wheeled in to the ultrasound room, other family members came until the chairs lining the walls were filled and still he paced, not caring if he looked like mad man, not giving a damn what they thought of him. He could not rest until he knew his family was safe.

So many thoughts flashed through his mind. What if the doctors had to choose between mother and child? What if he lost one of them? Or both? It didn't bear thinking about. God knew, he would give all his money, every single penny to know that they were both all right.

And if this was what love meant, then he loved them, Godammit. He loved Erin DeSouza and he loved his baby and he was making no apologies for it. He just prayed they'd both make it through so that he could show them how much he loved them.

He was at the point when he felt he would go mad with worry when he saw the doctor in his green scrubs heading down the hallway toward him. He didn't wait for him to get to him. He met him halfway, his eyes searching the doctor's face, trying to read the news that was to come.

"They're…okay?" His voice sounded strained even to his own ears. He could hardly speak. The anxiety was killing him.

The doctor sighed.

Dare almost had a heart attack. Jesus, a doctor sighing. That was not a good sign.

"They're both resting," he said with a small smile.

Dare let his breath out in a whoosh. They were alive. Both of them. That was a start. "Are they okay?" he asked again.

"Mommy is doing well," the doctor said, "but it was a difficult surgery. Baby was in a lot of distress."

Dare glared at the doctor. He was just inches from strangling the man. "What the hell does that mean? Is my baby okay or not?"

"Mr. DeSouza, please," the doctor said, putting up a hand. "There are other people-"

"I don't give a flying fig who else is here. Tell me what's going on with my baby."

"She's been taken to the intensive care unit to be placed in an incubator. She's only two pounds and needs to be placed in a protected environment."

She? Hadn't he heard 'he' somewhere? But it didn't matter either way. He just wanted his baby to be all right.

"Will she survive, doctor?" He kept his voice low, guilty at his previous outburst but still too concerned to worry about an apology.

The doctor pursed his lips. "Her chances are better than fifty percent but I don't want you to get your hopes up, just in case."

Better than fifty percent. It wasn't enough. He wanted to hear that she was perfectly fine, she'd be all right, she'd grow up and graduate from high school and give him all the grief that teenage girls gave their middle-aged dads. That was what he wanted to hear. But the doctor was giving him no such assurances so he clung to the only positive word he'd been given. Better. Better than fifty percent. He would hold on to 'better' and make it real.

"Can I see them now?" he asked.

The doctor nodded. "I'll take you to your wife. She's conscious but a bit groggy. You can see the baby afterwards."

Dare nodded and followed him down the hallway. He was taken to a private room where Erin lay in the bed, pale and quiet, her eyes closed. He pulled up a chair beside her and gently touched her arm. Her eyes opened and he could see her trying to focus. "Dare," she said, her voice weak and scratchy, "where's my baby? Is he all right?"

"It's a she, Erin," he said. "We have a daughter. She's in the ICU right now and they're taking good care of her."

"Is she going to be all right?" Erin's eyes searched his face, looking for the same assurance he'd just sought from the doctor.

He took her hand in his and gave it a gentle squeeze. "She's very tiny, Erin. Only two pounds but if she's anything like her mother she'll pull through all right."

"How?" Erin whispered. She looked up at him, her eyes full of distress. "How can she make it?"

"She will," Dare said, his voice firm with conviction. In his heart he knew that his daughter would be all right. They both would. Leaning over he kissed Erin on the forehead. "Just rest for a while. I'm going to check on her." Then he gave her a reassuring smile. "Start thinking of girl names till I get back."

With that Dare left her and headed to the intensive care unit. The nurses there were welcoming but they refused to let him go into the nursery.

"The babies in this section are very delicate," they told him. "Their immune systems aren't developed yet. We have to make it as sterile an environment as possible."

They took him to a wide glass window and it was from there that he got his first view of his daughter, so tiny and pink in her incubator, with a shock of dark brown hair that made him think of her mother. There were strings and tubes leading from her mouth, her nose and her arm and his heart ached at the little one's cold and sterile introduction to the world. He should be able to hold his daughter close right now. She should be lying on the comfort of her mother's breast. But she was all alone and so tiny. How would they even care for her?

But as he stared at her, so small but yet so beautiful in her cocoon of glass, he knew they'd find a way. The baby had done her part by bravely making her way into the world. Now it was time for him and for Erin to play their part.

"You're a fighter, little one," he whispered through the glass, "and we won't let you down."

***

Nearly eight weeks passed before Erin and Dare were allowed to take Soleil Denise DeSouza home from the hospital. By that time she weighed four pounds and had grown another inch. The nurses warned them she was a feisty one, kicking up a windstorm when she was ready to be fed and demanding to be held when it was naptime.

"You have to put your foot down," one of the nurses warned Erin, "or else she'll walk all over you. You need to show her who's in charge."

Erin smiled and thanked the nurse for her advice but when she looked into her daughter's big brown eyes how could she refuse her? She'd already been through so much in her little life that Erin could be excused for spoiling her a little bit, couldn't she?

And Daddy was even worse, jumping up at every cry, checking on the baby every hour of the night. Within a week he'd begun to look so ragged with exhaustion that Erin had to banish him from the nursery for an entire night just so he could get some sleep.

Through it all Francine was a savior. She knew all about babies, having raised three of her own plus a handful of grandkids. She guided Erin every step of the way through the feedings, burpings, bouts of colic and a brief period of jaundice. Finally the whole family settled into a comfortable rhythm - daddy, mommy, baby and adopted grandma - and finally Erin felt that her world was at peace.

Her love for Dare blossomed and she felt she could not love him more than she did right then. Each time she watched him holding Soleil, singing softly to her as she stared up at him with those adorable brown eyes, her heart swelled with pride and she couldn't help smiling. She'd come a long way but so had he. Who would have thought that bad boy billionaire Dare DeSouza could abandon his big shot image to play peek-a-boo and do goo-goo-gaa-gaa speak? She loved it, and in her eyes he was a bigger man for taking the time to amuse his baby.

And on top of all that he'd shown her nothing but love and respect, catering to her every need and going out of his way to make her feel loved. When he wasn't holding Soleil he was holding her, making her feel like the center of his world.

When Dare returned to work after Soleil had completed her second month it took Erin a while to adjust. She'd gotten so used to having him there that she couldn't help missing him. Still, she knew Dare's work was a big part of who he was. He loved what he did and she knew his work made him feel fulfilled. Besides, he had a lot to do on the last resort he'd bought so she needed to give him some space.

One evening as she sat feeding Soleil, Dare walked into the sitting room looking handsome as usual in his business wear. He gave her a peck on the cheek then kissed his daughter on the forehead.

"Guess what?" he said as he loosened his tie. "I got a call from your friend. She said she's been trying to reach you on your cell phone but all she keeps getting is your voice mail."

Erin's heart jerked. "My friend?"

"Yes, the one who came to visit. She's been trying to get in touch with you for the longest time. Did you disconnect your cell phone?"

"Ahh, no," she said, which was the truth. But it wasn't the whole truth. The fact was, she'd turned off her cell phone the day Soleil was born and had refused to turn it back on since then. She'd been living in a bubble of her own making. She'd done everything she could to insulate herself from the poison darts that Robyn could throw. But now she could see that her efforts had all been in vain. Robyn was determined to burst her bubble and send her reeling back to reality.

"Did she say what she was calling about?" Erin asked. It took all her effort to keep her face calm and her voice steady.

Dare shook his head. "No, but she left a number where you can reach her." He dug into his pocket and pulled out a slip of paper. He rested it on the table nearby and shifted the vase onto the edge of it to keep it from blowing away. "Give her a call as soon as you can," he said. "It sounds as if it's pretty important."

Erin pursed her lips. She knew exactly what was so important for Robyn. She was intent on ruining her life. But she would not give her the satisfaction of being the one to reveal her secret. She'd run away from her truth long enough and now she was tired of running.

"Dare," she said as she put the baby on her shoulder and gently rubbed her back, "we need to talk."

CHAPTER TWELVE

Dare looked at her, curious. "About what?" he asked. "Something to do with Soleil?" Then he grinned. "Has she been a naughty princess? I know she loves to boss her mommy around."

"No," Erin said, her voice solemn. "It's about me."

Dare frowned. "About you? Is everything all right?"

She shook her head. "No, but let me set the baby down for her nap and then we'll talk." Still rubbing Soleil's back she got up and headed for the nursery.

Dare stood there in the sitting room, confused. Erin had seemed so peaceful when he'd come in but now he could sense her agitation and it bothered him. It had something to do with this Robyn woman, he was sure. Her whole demeanor had changed at the mention of Robyn's name.

He threw off his jacket and dropped onto the sofa to await her return. He didn't have to wait long. Erin approached and her face was serious. Whatever she wanted to talk about was not going to be fun.

She sat in the chair across from him and folded her hands in her lap. She was so beautiful, with her dark hair curling around her face and onto her shoulders, and those hazel eyes that were so expressive. Now, though, they were clouded over with what looked like heartfelt pain. He sat up and reached for her hand but she pulled it back.

"What's going on, Erin? Is something wrong with you?" At her nod his heart jerked inside his chest. "Are you sick?"

She shook her head.

"Then what is it?" he demanded, beginning to lose patience. She had him on pins and needles and was taking her own sweet time in clearing up the mystery. "Just spill it."

She sighed. "All right, I will." She plucked at the fabric of her yellow sundress and then began to twist it with her fingers. Clearly, what she had to say was not easy for her. "I've not been honest with you, Dare. I'm not who you think I am."

His eyes narrowed as he stared at her. "What's that supposed to mean?"

She sucked in a deep breath then let it out slowly. "It means, when I tell you who I really am you'll probably want me out of your life. For good."

That gave him pause. What in the world could Erin have done to let her say something like that? He loved her. Couldn't she see that? There was nothing that could make him want her out of his life.

"Tell me," he said. "Let me be the judge."

She caught her bottom lip between her teeth and for several seconds she worried the lip until finally she opened her mouth to speak. And when she did, her voice was a hoarse whisper. "I know how important honesty is to you," she said. "You said it yourself. You said it was the most important thing to you in a friendship. And that's why I know you'll hate me for this."

"What are you talking about, Erin?"

"My parents died when I was twelve and I grew up in foster care." She'd begun wringing her sundress again. "I was moved from home to home and some of them were…awful." She gave a hiccup up at the last word. She seemed on the verge of tears. "At one of the homes, I had to struggle to survive. I often went without meals. Once, at school, I was so hungry I passed out."

Dare held his breath. He could already guess what she was about to say.

"One day I just cracked. I walked into a supermarket and filled a basket with everything I wanted then I sneaked into the bathroom and filled up my backpack," she whispered then put her fists to her mouth as a sob escaped her lips. "When I came out of the bathroom I tried sneaking out through the back, where the employees worked. I didn't know...I didn't know the alarm would go off. I thought that only worked at the front entrance. I ran. And then...and then they chased me down the alley and onto the main road. I ran and ran but I wasn't fast enough." She dropped her face in her hands and began to cry in earnest. "One of them grabbed me and I couldn't get away. He punched me then he shoved me to the ground. And he kicked me. Many times. And then...the police came."

Dare went over to kneel in front of her then he pulled her into his arms. "Hush, it's okay, honey. It's okay."

"No, it's not okay," she said, wrenching herself out of his arms. "I've lived with the guilt all these years. Before I married you I should have told you but I didn't have the courage. How could I tell you that you were marrying somebody who was charged with a criminal offense?"

"It wasn't your fault, Erin. You were a victim of your circumstances.."

She shook her head violently. "No, it was all my fault. I should never have done that. I...don't know what came over me."

"It's okay, honey. I don't hate you for what you did. We all make mistakes. It was wrong but...understandable under the circumstances." For a long while Dare was silent, just holding Erin, rocking her in his arms. Gradually her trembling ceased and her breathing calmed. Only then did he speak. "Robyn knew about this, didn't she? She used this information against you."

Her head still resting against his shoulder, Erin nodded. "She threatened to tell you everything. I'm guessing that's what today's call was about."

Dare put a finger under Erin's chin and lifted her face to his. "Know this, Erin DeSouza. I love you and there is nothing about you or your past that will make me stop."

Her eyes widened as she stared up at him. "Dare, what are you saying? You've never told me you loved me."

"I know. I was a fool. It was a secret I kept to myself but I'm telling you now. I love you, Erin. You and Soleil are my life. I want you with me forever."

Her face crumpled and he could see she was struggling to hold back the tears . "Do you mean it, Dare? Don't play with me."

"Do I look like I'm joking?" His grip tightened round her. "You're mine and you can keep digging up all the skeletons you want. You'll never scare me off. You're never going to get away from me, Erin. You're trapped with me on this island. I'll hide your passport if I have to."

To his relief that got him his first smile from her. "You won't have to," she said, smiling through her tears. "You have me for life."

And when Dare pulled her close and kissed her she responded with a passion that told him, without a doubt, that every word she said was true.

"Thank you so much for coming, Dare." Robyn clasped his hand for a second and her eyes brimmed with tears.

Then she turned to Erin. "And Erin how can I ever thank you?" She took a step forward and wrapped her arms around Erin in a fierce hug. Then she stepped back and dabbed daintily at her eyes with a handkerchief.

"I'm so glad you were able to make it for the funeral. Mom had a special place in her heart for you, Erin. You know that, don't you?" She dabbed at her nose then tucked her hankie into her purse. "That's why I was so distressed when I couldn't reach you. Mom would never have forgiven me." She looked over at Dare. "Did Erin tell you I was always jealous of her?" She gave a little laugh. "Mom was always comparing the two of us. Erin was the angel and I was the devil." She shrugged. "It took me a long time to realize what Mom wanted me to learn from Erin - her strength, her determination." Her eyes took on a faraway look. "During those last days in her battle with cancer we talked…more than we talked all my years growing up in the house. And that's when I began to understand her and how much she wanted the best for me."

She took a deep breath then pasted a brave smile on her lips. "I guess it's time for me to grow up now." She touched Erin on the shoulder then turned and walked across the churchyard to the limousine where the rest of her family waited patiently for her.

After she climbed into the car and they drove off Erin turned to her husband. "Thanks for coming with me," she said.

"I wouldn't have let you come alone," he said with a smile. "Now let's get back to the hotel before Princess Soleil drives poor Francine crazy."

With a chuckle he put his arms around her shoulder and Erin put her arm around his waist knowing that she had the greatest blessing in the world. She was loved.

Thank you for reading!

Free book offer: Get your free copy of 'Rome for the Holidays' by joining my mailing list. On signing up you will be provided with the link to the story. Just visit my website to join:

www.judyangelo.com

If you've already read this story and would simply like notification when I have new books out, still visit my website and click on the sign-up link to join my mailing list. You may then choose to ignore the link to the free book. When new stories are out I'll keep you posted.

www.judyangelo.com

If you wish to drop me a line, please send your e-mail to:

judyangeloauthor@gmail.com
.

I would love to hear from you!

Sneak Preview of the next in the series:

BAD BOY BILLIONAIRES SERIES
VOLUME 4

Dangerous Deception

CHAPTER ONE

"But Dani…"

"No 'buts'. Just tuck it away for a rainy day." Dani stuffed the bank notes into her brother's pocket.

"But where'd you get-"

"What did I tell you, Brian?" She shoved him toward the door. "Now go. I'll be right down. I just want to make sure we didn't forget anything."

As Brian exited the door, pulling the large suitcase behind him, Dani turned to look at the boxes still standing in the hallway. She shook her head. She had no idea how all that was going to fit into her Chevy Blazer. She'd warned her brother not to pack too many things but he was taking so much stuff that she almost felt like he was moving out for good and not just leaving Chicago to head out for his first semester at the University of Notre Dame. She went into the living room and then into the kitchen, looking around to see if he had left anything lying about. Finally, she went to his bedroom.

As she opened the door a flood of emotions filled her and she blinked quickly, fighting back the tears. This room had been Brian's haven for the last four years, ever since she had moved them to this apartment when their father died from a heart attack. She had been only eighteen years old but fortunately legally qualified to be Brian's guardian. Her mother succumbed to breast cancer when Brian was only eight and then they lost their dad when he was fourteen. She swore that as long as she had breath he would not lose her, too. He would never be placed in foster care. And she'd kept her promise.

Dani pulled the door closed and went to the living room where she picked up her handbag and slung it over her shoulder. As she went through the door she plastered a brave smile on her face. There was no way she was going to let Brian know how deeply she was affected by his leaving. He was ready to start his new life as a college student and she wanted nothing to distract him. She'd been a mother hen for the last four years but now she would just have to learn to let go.

She took the elevator to the ground floor then went out to the car and hopped into the driver's seat. She turned to her brother. "Ready to go?"

He shrugged. "As ready as I'll ever be."

She reached over and tousled his hair just like she used to do when he was six years old. "Then let's go get 'em, tiger."

****

Dani's first week without Brian was busy, which was a blessing for her. Her new schedule did not allow her the luxury of sitting at home feeling lonely. Each day she rushed home from her teaching job at Applewood Preschool, changed into her uniform for her new night job as chauffeur at Apex Limousine Company, and checked in for work by five o'clock sharp.

She'd been on the job five nights and so far had survived despite some rough spots. Tonight, though, something was different. She'd been summoned to the boss's office and through the glass door she could see Tony Martino, the owner and manager. He was pacing the floor. As she pushed the door open and entered his office he nodded to her.

"We need to talk," he said and jerked his head toward the only chair that did not have papers piled on top of it.

Dani's heart fell. Tony looked none too pleased. What had she done to upset him? She couldn't afford to lose this job, not right now. She'd only been working with the company a week and already had been able to send money to Brian for his books. She was counting on next week's pay to cover the cost of his hockey uniform.

He flopped down in the chair behind his desk then his look softened as he stared at her. "Don't look so worried," he said. "I'm not going to fire you."

Dani let out her breath slowly and cursed herself for having such an expressive face.

"I know you're wondering what this is all about," he said and leaned forward. "I heard about the incident the other night."

She held her breath again, sure she would be reprimanded for literally dumping one of her passengers on his own driveway. The man had been drunk and had tried to grope her as she held the door open to let him out. She'd pushed him off and, unsteady as he was, he'd landed on his behind. Now she was in trouble because of it. She looked back at her boss but remained silent.

Tony's face grew serious. "I heard about the incident through a third party and I'm not pleased. Why didn't you tell me what happened?"

Dani's glance wavered and she looked down at her hands. When she said nothing Tony spoke again, even more sternly. "From the day I interviewed you I could see you were a tough kid but you can't keep things like this a secret. You have to remember that you're a woman and you have to be careful." He leaned back and clasped his hands over his paunch. "And I have to remember that, too. I'm not proud of the fact that I put you in that situation."

Her eyes flew to his face. "But you didn't-"

"Yes, I did." He cut her off. "I should have known better than to give you a random assignment." He steepled his fingers and fixed her with a frown. "From now on you'll be assigned only to reliable customers. I'm going to give you a very important customer of mine. His father was my client for many years and now he uses my services, too." Tony paused as if for effect. "His name is Storm Hunter."

Dani frowned. "*The* Storm Hunter? Of the Hunter's Run clothing line?"

Tony nodded and gave her a satisfied smile. "The one and the same. I've been serving his family for over twenty-three years. I've known Storm since he was a kid." Then his face grew serious. "As I said, he's an important client. The Hunters, they've been good to me. It's not like they need my services that much but they always give me business. That's the kind of people they are."

"I understand and I'll take good care of him," she said, still slightly dazed. Imagine that. She'd be chauffeur to a member of the Hunter family, one of the wealthiest in the Chicago area. They were 'old money' and everyone knew of them. And even with all that money the oldest son, Storm, had branched out of the family's manufacturing business and had started his own clothing line, making himself a billionaire many times over at the ripe old age of twenty-seven.

"And seeing that you've already made some adjustments to your appearance I want you to keep it that way." He gave her a nod of approval. "I can't vouch for all my other customers so I don't necessarily want to broadcast that I have a woman on the team. You don't know who you might attract once that kind of information gets around." He stood up and walked over to check the computer sitting on the desk in the far corner. "Tonight you're going to pick up Mr. Hunter from a party and get him safely home. If he plans to drink he always arranges for us to come get him. You can check the location on your computer in the car."

This was Dani's cue to get going. She stood up and gave her boss a quick nod. "Thank you, sir. I appreciate your looking out for me."

"No problem, Swift. Now just grow some hair on that baby face of yours and look tough." Tony was chuckling as Dani walked out of his office and headed for the garage.

Things had turned out a lot better than she'd thought. There she was, thinking she was about to get fired, and instead she'd been assigned to a man who was probably the limousine company's most prestigious client.

Now if only his tips would be as big as his name, she'd be sweet.

That night Dani arrived on location a whole fifteen minutes before the appointed time. There was no way she would risk being late. And she'd prepared well, too, making sure to pile every last strand of her thick dark hair underneath the rim of the chauffeur's hat. She'd been doing that since the groping incident. She'd ditched the earrings and had left her face devoid of any form of make-up. She'd even practiced her walk, trying to eliminate the feminine sway of her hips and adopt instead the long strides of a man. Thank God she was taller than most of her sex. At five feet seven and a half she could easily pass for a man. Now if only she could grow some hair on her chin. She chuckled at the thought. She was willing to go far but not that far.

At five minutes after ten people started leaving the stately mansion. The cars that rolled out of the driveway included Porsches, Jaguars and a Bentley. Then there were others who chose to depart in limousines. Storm Hunter would be one of them.

Dani recognized him immediately. Over six feet tall and dangerously handsome, he was dressed in a designer suit of midnight black, his dark hair curling deliciously at the collar. He strode down the driveway toward her with an air of supreme confidence that almost took her breath away. He had billionaire stamped all over him.

Realizing she was staring she immediately straightened to her full height and masked her face with a stony expression. The last thing she wanted was for this man to think she was ogling him. Although, if ever there was a man to fit the description of 'eye candy', he was it. But she couldn't be caught staring. She had to remember she was a professional, she was on the job, and on this job she was a man. Sort of.

Storm Hunter was halfway to the car when a tall, willowy blonde ran down the driveway toward him.

"Storm, wait for me," she called in a light, airy voice. "I want to come with you."

For a fraction of a second Storm's brows fell and a look of annoyance passed over his face. Then it went blank and he turned to meet the woman who was now almost upon him. "Lola," he said, his deep voice quiet and cool, "I thought you were heading for home."

"I am," she said with a laugh as she caught his arm and clung to it. "Daddy didn't come for me as he promised so I'm hitching a ride with you." She looked up at him with huge eyes full of adoration then she added the finishing touch when she set her crimson lips in a teasing pout.

Dani almost gagged. Christ, the things some women did to get a man's attention. Then, realizing the direction of her thoughts, she made her face bland. It was not her place to judge or to get involved in the affairs of these people. Best to just focus on doing her job.

"My pleasure," Storm said but his voice was anything but pleasant. He'd spoken with a formality that made it clear that he would have preferred to travel alone.

The woman he'd called Lola didn't seem to notice his reticence. "Thank you so much, darling," she gushed. "Now we can get a chance to talk some more. You know Daddy loves it when we talk." Then she batted her eyes in what she must have thought was an irresistibly seductive manner.

Dani clenched her teeth to keep from uttering a sound. As tempted as she was to give a groan of disgust that was a luxury she could not afford. But honestly, the woman's simpering was past annoying. She didn't know how Storm Hunter could stand it.

He seemed to be handling it fairly well, though. They'd started walking toward the car and there was a slight smile on his lips, admittedly a somewhat sardonic-looking smile, but a smile nonetheless. The woman slipped a hand into the crook of his arm and he didn't seem to mind. They looked quite comfortable now as they strolled toward her.

But things aren't always as they seem, as Dani soon realized. To her surprise, when the couple got up close she saw the glint of irritation in the man's eyes and then he gave her a knowing look. For that nanosecond Dani's heart froze. Storm Hunter had just exchanged a look with her, a look that said he was pissed and he didn't mind letting her know because she would understand. It was one of those looks shared between men. Except, she wasn't a man.

But he didn't know that.

He was standing right in front of her now. Dani gave a quick nod of greeting, the perfect excuse for her to drop her gaze and break the hold of his stare. "Good evening, Mr. Hunter," she said in a low voice then leaned forward and opened the door of the limousine. Storm helped Lola then he bent his tall frame and climbed in, leaving Dani to close the door behind them. A moment passed before she could move. He'd been so close that the heady fragrance of his cologne filled her nostrils. That, combined with his nearness, had her heart racing like she'd just done a hundred meter sprint. Christ, what in the world was wrong with her?

The man was just a man, after all. True, but this was one handsome piece of man with his thick brows, square jaw and those deep dark eyes that seemed to bore a hole into her soul. He was the first man who'd made her breath catch in her throat. She'd gone through her fair share of romance novels and had read about heroes who stole your breath away but she'd never had that happen to her, had never even believed it. Until now.

She gave her head a quick shake. *Back to reality, Dani. You can't afford to go soft on a guy now. He's the client, remember?* Her emotions again under control, she strode back to the driver's seat and slid behind the wheel. She was calm now, almost able to laugh at herself. And she had a feeling she'd need a sense of humor.

If the last few minutes were anything to go by this was going to be an interesting journey.

Click here to get your copy:
Dangerous Deception

BAD BOY BILLIONAIRES
Volume 1 - Tamed by the Billionaire
Volume 2 - Maid in the USA
Volume 3 - Billionaire's Island Bride
Volume 4 - Dangerous Deception
Volume 5 - To Tame a Tycoon
Volume 6 - Sweet Seduction
Volume 7 - Daddy by December
Volume 8 - To Catch a Man (in 30 Days or Less)
Volume 9 – Bedding her Billionaire Boss
Volume 10 - Her Indecent Proposal
Volume 11 - So Much Trouble When She Walked In
Volume 12 – Married by Midnight

THE BILLIONAIRE BROTHERS KENT
Book 1 - The Billionaire Next Door
Book 2 - Babies for the Billionaire
Book 3 - Billionaire's Blackmail Bride
Book 4 - Bossing the Billionaire

THE CASTILLOS
Book 1 - Beauty and the Beastly Billionaire
Book 2 – Training the Tycoon
Book 3 – The Mogul's Maiden Mistress
Book 4 – Eva and the Extreme Executive

HOLIDAY EDITIONS
Rome for the Holidays (Novella)
Rome for Always (Novel)

The NAUGHTY AND NICE Series
Volume 1 - **Naughty by Nature**

COMEDY, CONFLICT & ROMANCE Series
Book 1 - Taming the Fury
Book 2 - Outwitting the Wolf
Book 3 – Romancing Malone

COLLECTIONS
BAD BOY BILLIONAIRES, Coll. I - Vols. 1 - 4

Author contact:
www.judyangelo.com
judyangeloauthor@gmail.com

Author contact:
judyangeloauthor@gmail.com

Connect with me on Facebook:
Judy Angelo Author

Cover Artist: Ramona Lockwood (Covers by Ramona)

Printed in Great Britain
by Amazon

18741910R00142